VOLUME TWO

AIRSHIP 27 PRODUCTIONS

AN AIRSHIP 27 PRODUCTION

Bass Reeves Frontier Marshal Volume 2
"Ambush at Cold River" © 2017 Milton Davis
"Train Robbery" © 2017 Mel Odom
"The Pledge" © 2017 Michael Black
"The Bixbee Breakout" © 2017 Derrick Ferguson

Published by Airship 27 Productions
www.airship27.com
www.airship27hangar.com

Interior illustrations © 2017 Rob Davis
Cover illustration © 2017 Marco Turini

Editor: Ron Fortier
Associate Editor: Fred Adams Jr.
Marketing and Promotions Manager: Michael Vance
Production and design by Rob Davis.

ISBN-10: 1-946183-19-9
ISBN-13: 978-1-946183-19-4

Printed in the United States of America

10 9 8 7 6 5 4 3 2 1

BASS REEVES
FRONTIER MARSHAL
VOLUME 2
CONTENTS:

PAGE 5
1875
AMBUSH AT COLD RIVER
BY MILTON DAVIS

Bass Reeves and Quickshot Katy come to the aid of a group of black settlers being chased by a vengeance-seeking former Confederate Officer.

PAGE 47
1877
TRAIN ROBBERY
BY MEL ODOM

Marshal Reeves and his posseman trail a murderous train robber to the quiet little town of Venita. There he goes undercover to learn the identity of his prey and the real reason behind the crime.

PAGE 95
1879
THE PLEDGE
BY MICHAEL BLACK

To honor his promise to a dying lawman, Bass Reeves takes on a gang of outlaws intent on robbing an Army gold shipment.

PAGE 142
1894
THE BIXBEE BREAKOUT
BY DERRICK FERGUSON

Bass and his deputies hole up in a small town jail with their prisoners hoping to hold off the rest of the gang without any help from the frightened townspeople.

Ambush at Cold River

By Milton Davis

The deer stumbled through the dry brush, scrounging for forage. The weather had been harsh of late, leaving little for beast or man. It showed in the animal's body, its skin close to its bones. A bark of a Winchester ended the deer's suffering; it stumbled a few feet then collapsed onto the dry grass.

Katy Calhoun lowered the rifle from her shoulder then frowned. On any other season she would have let the sickly deer pass, waiting for something more substantial. But times were hard this season. The drought had yet to break and the land suffered. Beggars can't be choosers, the saying goes, and while Katy wasn't near to begging she was close to taking on a less respectable profession if things continued to get worse.

She was about to scramble down the hill to claim her kill when she heard voices on the opposite side of the valley. She crouched and brought her rifle back to her shoulder. She spotted the first man creeping toward her kill, a Colt in his hand. Two more men flanked him to the right, two more to the left. A sixth man hung back, standing still with a rifle at his shoulder as he scanned the hillside. Katy crouched lower, hoping to hide from his gaze.

"Whoever you are, we appreciate you sharing this deer with us," the man shouted.

Katy's temper got the best of her.

"Who the hell said I was sharing?"

She moved as soon as she spoke, working her way back behind the hill.

"Well now," the man replied. "Looks like we have a little lady to thank.

5

If you just hold on for a minute we'll come and thank you personally."

Katy scanned the hillside, taking a moment to mark each man's position.

"How about you come on out in the open and make this..."

Katy's first shot sent the talker scurrying for cover. Her second shot smashed into the forehand of the man closest to her, knocking him back into a sapling oak. Her third shot caught one of the men to her right in the gut. He clutched the wound as he fell to his knees cursing.

She was moving when the others began shooting back. Common sense would have told her to fall back behind the hill, get on her horse and ride away. But Katy was angry, and when she was angry somebody had to feel it. She was also heeding the words her parents told her long ago. Once you shoot at a person they're not your friend anymore. They're your enemy, and a person is only an enemy as long as they're alive.

Katy fired another round at the talker, keeping him behind his tree. She fell to the ground as the branches above her head were shot into splinters. Katy didn't return fire. She waited in the prone position, her rifle sighted. The other men finally appeared creeping toward her, their sidearms drawn.

"Did we kill her?" one of them asked.

"I think so," the other answered.

"What a waste," the third man said. "We could've had us some fun before we killed her."

Katy bit her lip. She waited until they were in full view.

"Hey!" she yelled.

Katy gunned the men down before they could pull their triggers.

She checked to see if the talker was still lurking on the hill before rising to her feet and walking to the three still bodies. All three were dead; Katy fired three bullets into their heads to make sure.

"Goddamn trash," she said.

A revolver fired and a bullet whizzed by her head. Katy fired back in reflex.

"Shit!" the talker yelled.

Katy chased the talker, running up the hill to its crest. As he reached the summit the talker shot at her again, striking the tree nearby. She flattened on the ground, her rifle aimed from the prone position as she searched for him. After a few moments she sprang to her feet, working from tree to three as she searched for him.

"Yah!" she heard him shout. Katy saw the man riding off. She tried to draw a bead on him but the trees blocked a clear shot. She slowly lowered her gun then shook her head.

"I'll see you again," she said. "You can count on it."

She sauntered down the hill, stopping to go through the pockets of the men she killed. No reason to leave anything valuable with them. They wouldn't need it. She collected twenty dollars, four watches and a flask of whiskey. She had planned to dress the deer on the spot, but that was no longer an option. The shootout may have been heard by others so her best bet was to take what she could from the deer and leave the rest to the woods. She knew a Cherokee that would pay good money for the horses and saddle, no questions asked. The rest belonged to her. She'd have to go into Felicity for supplies which she had hoped to avoid. For a brief moment she felt remorse but it quickly dissipated. Get or get got, that's what her parents always said. Today she got.

She took out her knife, cut the flank portion from the beast then tied it in place. Katy was not a small woman, standing taller than most men and possessing a full bosom and wide hips. She kept her hair cut short in a black curly mass on her head. A solitary life made her just strong as most men as well. She would ride a few miles north before stopping to set up camp for the night. In the morning she would head for Felicity. Once again she had blood on her hands. She was sure it wouldn't be the last.

Bass Reeves tipped back his hat as he scanned the open grass field before him. He was looking for signs to tell him he was headed in the right direction. He'd been tracking the Bowden Gang for six days, keeping a safe distance all the while. They were moving fast, which told him they knew they were being followed. He finally spotted the trail, a ragged path of broken grass that skirted the field between the grass and the forest. The trail led to a narrow path into the woods that weaved through the new growth, probably a path tread by the few buffalo that remained in the area. The signs indicated the gang had passed this way at least a week ago. Bass wasn't making up any time. He'd have to forgo a few nights sleep if expected to catch up with them or hope they took a rest or two in the next few days. It was possible they would; they couldn't keep up the pace that long.

At midday he stopped to rest and eat. There was no time for a fire and a meal so the chewed on strips of jerky and washed them down with the warm water in his canteen. He gave his horses a few minutes to forage then set out on the trail again. For a few minutes he lost the trail, but picked it up again on the banks of a small creek skirting the edge of a steep hill.

As he stopped to fill his canteen Bass looked up to see buzzards circling overhead. At first he dismissed it, but then he decided to check it out. He mounted a fresh horse then travelled over the hill. The smell of death reached him as he crested the summit, growing stronger as he descended the opposite side. Sign was everywhere; there had been a gunfight. He came across the first body halfway down the slope. The man lay on his back, staring into the sky. It was definitely one of the Bowden boys. Bass dismounted then inspected the body. Not only had he been killed, he'd been robbed as well.

"Ain't that a turn," Bass said aloud, a grin lifting his voluminous mustache.

He found four more bodies close by. Each man had been robbed of valuables. There was a deer carcass nearby as well, the flank of the beast missing. Based on the bullet wounds Bass suspected the bandits had come across a hunter and expected to relieve him of his meal and probably his valuables. Apparently that hunter turned the tables on them then fled, which was why he took only a portion of the deer. Bass took the folded wanted poster from his pocket then matched the faces on the poster to those of the dead men on the hill. Despite early decomposition he was able to match them. One man was missing, Tom Bowden. He was the most wanted of the three and the man with the highest bounty. Knowing Bowden he sent his minions after the hunter as he sat back to provide cover, which is why he managed to escape.

It was messy work. Bass had no way of transporting the bodies; whoever killed and robbed the gang took their horses as well. He took items from each man to confirm their deaths then searched the area for more sign. Someone traveling with five horses was sure to leave a trail and it didn't take long to find it. Bass decided to follow the trail to see where it led. He would find the person who did this work and thank him or arrest him. He hadn't decided which. He'd make up his mind once he caught him.

Reverend Percival Stills bent over the shallow creek then cupped his calloused hands, dipping them into the warm water. He took a sip before washing his face and hands the best he could. He shook away the excess water then dried his hands on his pants. He stood, extending his full six foot frame then stretched out his arms. He turned and the burden of his task resettled on his broad shoulders. The others mingled about the wagons, waiting for his return so he could bless the supper. Percival insisted on washing up alone, one of the few times he had a moment to himself. He closed his eyes then bowed his head.

"Dear Lord Almighty, to you I give all praises. Thank you for protecting me with your everlasting grace, and thank you for blessing me with the task ahead."

He hesitated before continuing his prayer, uncertain if he should say what he was about to say. But if he could not share with the Lord, who could he share with? He dropped to his knees.

"Lord, sometimes I wonder why you laid such a task before me. I'm a young man. I ain't never had this kind of responsibility. There be folks in our group that could be my mammy or pappy, yet they look to me as if I'm their elder. I don't know how to handle that, dear Lord. These folks are trusting their lives with me, and I ain't sure I can deliver. But I'm going to trust in the vision you sent me. I'm going to put my faith in your hands. Whatever happens was meant to be. Amen."

Percival dusted off his knees and trotted back to his caravan/ congregation. His petite and beautiful wife, Precious, greeting him with mock consternation.

"Well it's about plumb time!" she said. "The stew is getting cold! I thought I was going to have to come and box your ear!"

The others laughed as Percival sauntered up to his wife then scooped her up into his arms then lifted her high.

"I'm your husband, not your child, Mrs. Stills," he said.

Precious smiled then kissed his forehead.

"Put me down and bless this food, Reverend!"

Percival placed down his bride then held her hand.

"Everybody join hands," he said.

Percival scanned the circle. Fifty-seven people stood in the circle. When they left Mississippi four months ago there were sixty-six. Six took sick and died; two died by accident and one disappeared. It was those deaths that burdened him, members of his congregation at the little church in Natchez that believed his vision and followed him out to this new wilderness for a better life. He never regretted what he left behind; a life not much different from slavery lived under the persecution of hooded white men. Edward Jenkins, the colored speculator that came to his house that evening with the words and the land deeds was like an angel to his prayers. Percival wasn't a fool; he made sure that what Edward offered was true. Once he confirmed that the land would belong to his congregation he set about in earnest earning the money to pay for the land and the supplies they would need to make the journey. The most precarious part was slipping away from their obligations to the men who owned the land they tilled. A plan was shared and a meeting place agreed upon, and in two days the congregation gathered and set out on their way.

The last man to join the circle was not a member of his congregation, a man that Percival and the others depended on despite not knowing much about him. Jason Jones was a man of righteous violence; a person that did what needed to be done for those without the will or bravery to do it. A union cap rested on his head and he wore the old jacket with its insignia from the war. Percival thought that Jason was still fighting that war, which is why he volunteered to guide the congregation to their Oklahoma paradise. Three days after they set out the landowners set riders after them to bring them back. Jason rode out to delay them. What he did he never spoke of nor was he asked. It was in the Lord's hands, Percival thought.

"Let's bow our heads," the reverend said. "Dear Lord, please bless this food we are about to receive and bless the hands of those who prepared it. In Jesus' name we pray. Amen."

"Amen," the congregation repeated.

The congregation lined up before the large iron cauldron where the stew simmered, spreading its savory aroma throughout the camp. Precious went to the cauldron, using the large ladle to scoop out the mixture of meat and vegetables. Percival took his place at the end of the line as always. To his surprise Jason joined him.

"Not much of that left," he said.

"I know," Percival replied.

"Not much around here as far as game either," Jason continued. "Looks like the drought done took its toll."

They kept pace with the line as they continued to talk.

"We're down to the last of our livestock," Percival said. "We'll have to go into the next town and buy supplies."

"I was hoping we could avoid that, but I guess you're right," Jason agreed reluctantly.

The reverend looked at the hard man and smiled.

"You have to trust people sometimes, Jay. You have to trust God."

Jay sucked his teeth then patted his revolver.

"I trust that God gave me the talent to use this," he said. "We fought a war and things ain't got no better, just different."

"You don't believe in what we're doing?"

Jay looked away. "I want to, reverend. I really do. But I've seen too much.

Done too much. I'm taking y'all where you need to go because I was paid to, and I'm a man of my word."

Jason's doubt stirred the same feeling in Percival. He closed his eyes and said a silent prayer before replying.

"I'm disappointed, Jay. I really am. The Lord gave me this charge and I'm seeing it through. I wish you would believe, too."

They stood before the kettle. Jason extended his bowl and Precious filled it.

"I don't have to believe in what you do," Jason said. "I just need to do my job, and I will. I can promise you that you'll get to your promised land. After that, I guess it's in God's hands."

Percival and Precious watched Jason amble away. They looked at each other with the same worried expression.

"Some of the congregation is feeling like him," Precious said.

"Let's not talk about it now," Percival suggested.

"We need to talk about it soon," his wife retorted. "You need to talk to them about it soon. Tonight. After supper."

"Yes ma'am," Percival said.

Precious smiled then filled his bowl. Afterwards she made a bowl for herself.

"Now come sit with your wife and let's enjoy what God has blessed us with."

Together they strolled to their wagon, sharing encouraging smiles with their flock. Percival pushed away the doubts of the day, strengthened by the hopeful faces. It wasn't a matter of whether he would lead them right.

After supper Sister Jane led the congregation in a round of songs, lifting everyone's mood, including Percival. He missed his old piano in Natchez; the instrument was too cumbersome to make the long journey. He promised the first thing he would do when they reached their new home was find and purchase a piano. Instead he played his banjo, the first instrument he learned to play, the instrument passed down to him from his daddy and his grandpa. Story was their first ancestor brought it all the way from Africa, but that was hard to believe seeing that most of the men and women that survived the journey across the ocean were packed naked and in close quarters. His mind was drifting back to grim thoughts, so he played with more gusto and sang as loud as his voice would allow. After the singing he gave a short sermon, actually more akin to an extended prayer. Feeling that all hearts and minds were satisfied, he and Precious retired to their wagon.

That night Precious allowed him to come to her side of the wagon. They made slow and gentle love, their muted voices masked by the breeze through the rustling leaves. Afterwards they held each other close, Percival fingers teasing Precious's hair, her fingers strumming his back.

"You're a good man, Percy," she whispered.

"Thank you," he said. "It makes me feel good to know I made you feel good."

Precious giggled then slapped his shoulder.

"I'm not speaking of me! I'm speaking of what you're doing for the congregation."

Percival rolled onto his back as he placed his hand behind his head.

"Sometimes I think I'm not the right person," he confessed.

"Nonsense! The Lord gave you this vision and He's never wrong. We're almost there and you're the one who led us this far. Soon we'll have our own land, and we'll build houses and raise our children in real freedom."

Percival's eyes widened and he shifted onto his side to gaze at his lovely wife.

"Family? Is there something you need to tell me?"

Precious shook her head. "Not yet. But I'm hoping once we reach home and get settled that children won't be far behind. It's time you and I started making some babies."

"We sure have been trying," Percival grinned.

Precious swatted his shoulder again.

"Hush up now, Percy. I'll not tolerate saloon talk in my bedroom."

"Why don't we quit talking and get back to trying to make that family?"

Precious wrapped her arms around his neck then pulled him on top of her and between her legs."

"I think that's a good idea, Percy," she whispered. "A splendid idea."

Morning came late for the couple as they tried to steal a few more minutes alone together. However the day wouldn't be denied, Percival dressed then went out to meet the congregation, walking among the wagons and checking to make sure everyone was in the best of spirits. It was later that morning when his hopes for a good day were dashed. Precious came to him, a worried look on her face.

"There will be no breakfast this morning," she said. "We don't have flour for biscuits and we're low on grits. We need supplies, Percival."

Percival placed his hands on his waist as he shook his head.

"Lord, you didn't mean for this to be easy, did you?"

He looked up at his wife and smiled.

"Precious, go back to the wagon and get me the money," he said. "I'm going to talk to Jay."

He found Jay at the edge of camp perched on his horse and scanning the horizon. The trail master spoke to him without looking.

"Morning, Reverend."

"Morning, Jay. Look, I need you to do some hunting today. We're low on food."

"Been hunting for days," Jay reminded. "This drought done killed just about everything nearby."

"Can you please try again?" Percival asked. "And take some of the men with you. They need to be busy."

Jay looked down at the reverend. "And what do you plan on doing. You're a good shot, better than most in the camp."

"I'm going into Felicity to see if I can get some supplies."

Jay frowned. "That's not wise."

"This ain't like Mississippi," the reverend said.

"How about I get those men and we all ride into Felicity together, just in case somebody wants to take issue about us being there?"

"No. Best I go alone. If this is like Mississippi, a group of armed Negroes riding into town is not going to sit well with the townsfolk. One reverend riding alone and unarmed won't stir no trouble."

"You ain't taking a gun?"

"No," Percival said, his voice conveying more confidence than he felt.

"I'm not bound to let that happen."

Jay jumped off his horse. He took one of his revolvers from his holster then stuck it in the front of Percival's pants.

"I think it's damn foolish to go into that town alone, but you're the boss. Since you hired me to protect this train, I'm going to protect it. You keep this gun hidden. Don't use it unless you need to."

Percival touched the handle of the Colt. It had been a long time since he held a pistol in his hand. Memories came to mind, memories that no one alive knew of from a life no one needed to be aware of.

"I'll take it," he said. "But I won't use it."

Jay climbed back on his horse. "I've done my job. I'll see you when you get back, reverend. If you come back."

"The Lord is my shepherd, Jay," Percival declared.

He turned then strode back his wagon to get his horse, reciting the 23rd Psalm on the way.

Bass rode into the tiny town of Buffalo Ford about midday. Buffalo Ford was less a town than a destination, a place where supplies could be had in between stretches of wild country. Anchoring the meager property was Cherokee Joe's Trading Post. Bass figured he'd ask a few questions here. Whoever took those horses probably brought them to Joe's to sell. Joe wasn't his real name; he didn't care for anyone not of the tribe knowing it. Joe also wasn't the type of person to ask questions. If you had to get rid of something fast, you came to Joe.

The crowd gathered around the entrance began to disperse as Bass approached. He wasn't hiding his identity as he normally did, his marshal badge on display. Bass tipped his hat to the men and women. Reclaiming stolen goods wasn't his job unless it was stolen from the Federal government and what most of these folks possessed was petty theft. Oklahoma, like most new territories, didn't turn out to be the Promised Land most folks imagined. If you had a little money and a lot of grit you could make a decent home of it. If not, then you might find yourself on the wrong side of the law.

Bass hitched his horses then took off his hat as he strode into the trading post. Cherokee Joe looked at him with a knowing smile as he entered.

"I knew it was you," he said. "Don't nobody scatter a flock of thieves like Bass Reeves."

"Howdy, Joe," Bass greeted. "Sounds like you trying to be a poet."

Joe let out a hardy laugh. "Not in English. What brings you to Buffalo?"

Bass leaned on the counter. "I've been tracking the Bowden gang for a few days. You heard of them?"

Joe snarled. "Yeah, I've heard of them. Nasty sons of bitches."

Bass nodded. "Well, I found five of them shot dead in the valley a few miles away from here."

"Good!" Joe spat on the floor to emphasize his feelings.

"I agree. Problem is there were six of them."

Joe nodded. "That one will be harder to track than six. Any idea who killed them?"

"No," Bass admitted. "I thought you could tell me. Their horses and their gear were gone. I thought somebody may have come here looking to make quick money."

"Now that's justice," Joe said. "Murderers and robbers got murdered and robbed. No, ain't nobody been through here with that kind of haul."

Bass's eyes narrowed. "You sure about that, Joe?"

Joe leaned over the counter and met Bass's hard gaze. "I'm positive, Marshal."

The crowd began to disperse as Bass approached.

"Wouldn't be the first time you lied to me, Joe."

Joe leaned back and chuckled. "No, it wouldn't be. But I give you my word this time. Nobody's been through with five horses or any gear."

Bass nodded. Joe was probably telling the truth. He reached into his pocket then tossed a penny on the counter.

"Give me a piece of that licorice."

Joe picked up the penny then stuffed it in his pocket. He went to the candy jar then returned with a strip of licorice, handing it to Bass. Bass bit into the candy before speaking again.

"Is the Sutter house still for rent?"

"Yep," Joe replied. "Just had to run a couple of folks out. They got me mixed up with a charity."

Bass took two silver dollars from his pocket then placed them on the counter.

"I think I'll hang around for a few days just in case somebody shows up."

Joe frowned. "That's going to be bad for my business."

"I'll make it up to you," Bass promised. "If I catch whoever it is stole the Bowden horses I'll recommend you get part of the reward."

Joe grinned. "That sounds reasonable."

Joe took the dollars, strolled back into his shop then returned with the keys to the Sutter house.

"Make yourself at home, marshal."

Bass took the keys and turned to leave.

"Much obliged," he said.

As he unhitched his horses one word lingered in his head. Home. Bass was used to being on the trail hunting down ne'er do wells, but this hunt taxed him more than most. When he set out his wife Nellie was pregnant and he hated leaving her in that condition. He wanted to wrap this case up as soon as possible, and whoever killed those five men helped him along. He still had to find Tom Bowden, and like he mused earlier the killer would be harder to track on his own.

The old Sutter home sat on top of a modest hill due east of the trade store. Joe built three homes in the area to serve as respites for folks who traveled a long way to trade and had the means to pay for lodging. The Sutters were one of the few families that took up residence, eventually working for Joe doing various odd jobs, legal and illegal. After the parents died three years ago of fever the children packed up and headed east. The home returned to its original status and was used as a field office by Bass whenever he was in the area, which was quite frequently.

Bass took his horses around the back of the home to the worn stables. There was fresh hay inside, which the horses took to immediately. Bass unloaded his gear then took it inside. He checked the woodshed then frowned; he would have to either chop wood before he settled or go back down the hill and get a few logs from Joe. At least there was a well. Bass was lowering the bucket into it when he felt something hard press against his back.

"I got you now, nigger!" a gruff voice said.

Bass closed his eyes as he recognized the voice.

"Billy Swayne," he said. "When did you get out?"

Bill Swayne pushed the revolver barrel into Bass's back.

"Shut up! Ain't nobody give you permission to talk!"

Billy took his guns from his holster then dropped them on the ground.

"You don't know how long I've been waiting for this day," Billy said. "I served five years because of you."

"You served five years because you broke the law," Bass said.

Pain exploded on Bass's head and he fell to one knee.

"I told you not to…"

Bass pivoted on his knee, wrapping his arms around Billy's knees. Billy's revolver went off and Bass's ears rang as he lifted the man off his feet, turned again then dumped him down the well. He didn't hear Billy splash into the water below as he stumbled away, shaking his head to get his hearing back. A warm trickle down his neck told Bass he's almost lost his life, but almost was a good word this day. Bass ambled back to the well. He could barely see Billy's body, but he knew there was no way he was getting him out. Billy Swayne had traded a hard cell for a wet grave. Bass said a quick prayer for the hapless man and for dodging death one more time. He touched his wound; it was a graze and would probably heal soon. He went to the barn and saddled a horse. There would be no water from that well for quite some time.

Katy guided her small herd up the slope leading to Buffalo Ford and Cherokee Joe's. Joe was the only person she knew that would give her a fair trade for the horses and gear, no questions asked. As she neared the building she noticed the area before the trade store was uncharacteristically empty. That could mean only one thing; there were lawmen about. Still, she had to get rid of the horses and Joe was the only person that could do it. She decided to take the risk.

Katy rode up to the store, hitched the horses then strode inside. She was about to walk up the stairs when Joe rushed outside, his eyes wide.

"Get those damn horses out of here!" he warned.

Katy didn't hesitate. She unhitched the horses then galloped away with them. She caught the expression on Joe's face, which meant he'd meet her later at a prearranged spot. This wasn't the first time she'd delivered something to him of questionable origin. The two of them had a history, one that Joe tried to rekindle whenever she came around. That was done; Joe was interesting but Katy was easily bored with men.

She arrived at the meeting place, a dense stand of oaks ideal for hiding from passersby on the nearby road. It was almost nightfall when Joe finally arrived.

"What took you so damn long?" Katy asked.

"I was trying to keep you from being arrested, that's what," Joe explained. "Bass Reeves is here and he's looking for those horses."

Katy grimaced. "How do you know he's looking for these horses?"

"I'll bet you a dollar you killed five men to get them," Joe said. "One of them got away."

"It didn't happen exactly like that."

Joe shrugged. "It doesn't matter. You took out the Bowden gang. Bass has been tracking them for a few weeks. You did him a favor, but he's going to be wondering why you didn't turn those horses in."

"Because they're mine," Katy said. "Bass will be okay with that. We know each other."

"Bass ain't nobody's friend when it comes to the law. Anyway, let's see what you got."

Joe inspected the horses then took a look at the gear.

"I'll give you one hundred and fifty dollars for the whole lot," Joe offered.

"One fifty! That's robbery, Joe. The horses are worth two hundred alone!"

"If this was legitimate business they would be, but it's not."

"Two hundred and I won't shoot you," Katy countered.

Joe began to smile, but Katy's expression stopped him.

"Okay, two hundred." He reached into his pocket and pulled out a wad of money.

"I don't want that. I want gold."

"You think I would walk around with that much gold?"

Katy's eyes narrowed. "Gold, Joe. You know I don't trust that paper money. If you ain't got it on you go back to the store and get it."

"I got it, I got it," Joe said. He reached into his other pocket and took out a pouch. He tossed it to Katy. She caught the pouch then opened it.

"Looks like enough," she said. "Nice doing business with you."

"Where you headed from here?" Joe asked.

"Not saying," Katy replied. "Don't want you letting anything slip around Reeves just in case there's a bounty on my head."

"You're a smart woman," Joe smiled. "Pretty, too."

Katy smirked as she mounted her horse.

"Get that image out your mind, Joe. We had our dance. It's been over."

She kicked her horse and set off down the trail.

"See you soon?" Joe called out.

"Not likely," Katy waved back. She guided her horses to the main road then galloped south. She still needed supplies. She could get them from Joe but she didn't want to linger, especially with Bass nearby. She would have to go to the closest town, one she'd rather not visit but had no choice. She was going to Felicity.

Tom Bowden cleaned the remaining syrup from his plate with his biscuit. He took his time eating the last of his breakfast, savoring the sweet taste. It was the first hot meal he had enjoyed in days. He chewed the last bite slowly then washed it down with black coffee.

"That was a mighty fine meal," he said. "Mighty fine."

Tom Bowden spoke to himself. The middle-aged woman who prepared the meal lay face down on the floor, blood oozing from under her body. Her husband lay on his back near the door, a bullet hole in his forehead. Tom had no intention of killing them, but when the farmer rushed in the door lowering his shotgun Tom acted on reflex. He knew the old man was suspicious of him when he rode up. He had started to turn back and find another place to rest. But he was tired of hiding in the woods and practically starving so he took a chance. Turned out to be a bad one.

Tom rose from the table. He searched the cupboards, taking whatever he could use on the road. He searched the farmer's body and then his wife for any valuables they might be carrying, and then searched the barn for any they might be hiding. It was sparse pickings. Like most farmers what they owned was in the soil. He tied the burlap bag closed, climbed onto his horse then rode across the barren fields into the woods. He had to stay off the main roads until he knew he was safe. He was sure if that bitch was following him but he wasn't taking any chances. Three days had passed and he still had a hard time believing what happened. Five good men dead in moments, shot down by a woman. His hand went to the red crease just above his left ear. A whisper to the right and he'd be just as dead as the rest of them. He hadn't seen shooting like that since…since Bass Reeves. Bile burned his throat as he thought of that damned US marshal, the man who was tracking him. His instincts told him not to hit the bank in Rochester, but greed and the urgings of his gang ruled over common sense. Turned out they'd stolen a federal payroll, which meant Reeves and the other marshals in the territory would be after them. They came to a quick decision; they'd make a run for Mexico, exchanging the money for gold before crossing the border. Instead, Michael Grossman, one of their gang, turned out to have his own plan. He took the money and disappeared, leaving Tom and the other six gang members broke. When they finally tracked Grossman down and killed him the money was nowhere to be found. They were back to the beginning, back to petty robberies and stealing, still intent on heading south. And then they ran into her.

Tom stuck to the wooded trails and paths for the next few days, keeping clear from any major roads. After two more days the solitude and wild game took its toll. He wasn't spending another minute in the woods. He worked his way to the main road, determined to follow it wherever it led. He was taking a stand. If the bitch or Bass Reeves still wanted him, then they would get him.

By the time Tom came across a town he was nearly starving. It was a modest place; a few office buildings opposite each other on a narrow, dusty street. On the left side was the general store; the right side the saloon. Tom headed straight for the saloon. He hitched his horse then pushed his way through the swinging doors. The innards of the establishment were as sparse as the town. A few local farmers played checkers at one of the tables, the others in the room empty. The bartender eyed him suspiciously as he cleaned glasses. There wasn't much of a selection of spirits occupying the shelves behind him, but Tom wasn't picky. He'd take what he could afford.

Tom nodded to the bartender as he leaned on the counter.

"What'll you have, stranger?" the barkeep asked.

"Whiskey, straight," Tom replied.

The barkeep poured him a shot which Tom downed quickly.

"What's your name, barkeep?"

"Silas Jones," the barkeep answered. "And who might you be?"

"Josey Wales," Tom said. "Say, where can a man find a decent room and a decent meal?"

"As you can see Felicity ain't a big town," Silas said. "Miss Laney rents a room at her house right outside of town. As far as a good meal, you can get one here if you got the gold."

"Give me another," Tom said.

The barkeep's eyes narrowed. "You ain't paid for the first."

Tom reached into his pocket took out a silver dollar then slammed it on the counter.

"That should pay for it, and one more," he said.

The barkeep filled his glass. Tom finished his drinks then headed for Miss Laney's house, studying the town as he rode. Wasn't much to it, but it was probably enough. As he rode up to the modest home the front door opened and a tall broad woman stepped onto the porch. Tom tipped his hat and the woman nodded back.

"I'm assuming you're Miss Laney," Tom said.

"That'd be me," the woman replied in a voice that seemed too small for her frame.

"The barkeep told me you might have a room to rent."

Miss Laney folded her arms across her ample breasts.

"I don't usually rent rooms to men who frequent saloons. They're usually troublemakers."

Tom dismounted then hitched his horse. As he walked up to the porch Miss Laney reached inside her door then pulled out a twelve gauge shotgun. Tom grinned; *now that's a smart woman.*

"If I was to start trouble it wouldn't be where I lived," Tom said as he extended his hand. "Name's Josey Wales."

Miss Laney looked at his hand then back to him.

"I got a free room out back over the barn. Fifty cents a day plus meals. Supper's on the stove now. I'll take two days rent up front."

"No rooms available inside?"

"None for you," Miss Laney declared.

Tom laughed so hard Miss Laney was forced to smile.

"I like you," he said. "I bet your husband does, too."

"He did when he was alive."

Tom paid Miss Laney then headed around back to the barn. The people of Felicity were a wary sort. He would have to be as well. He'd give the town two days, three days at the most. Then he would hit the bank, the saloon and head south.

Colonel Wilson Pickett lit his pipe then took a deep pull, savoring the flavor of imported Cuban tobacco. He looked down the rise on which he was perched as his companions guided their horses up the twisting trail. They were tired and had every right to be. The colonel set a hard pace. The task they were on was of upmost importance, one that had to be handled with alacrity. They were setting an example for others to follow.

Pickett was a Colonel in name only. He'd served four proud years in the Confederate Army, giving up his position as overseer of one of the largest plantations in Mississippi to fight the Union aggressors and preserve a way of life that had sustained his family for generations. Although he was the son of people of lesser means, dedication, valor and attrition found him with the rank of Colonel. His glorious war years ended at the Battle of Atlanta, where he was captured and forced into labor, following Sherman's vile march to Savannah; a campaign that sealed the fate of the South's grand vision. When he returned home he returned to a devastated land ruled by the same people he fought to keep in chains. For years he suffered in silence as Yankee carpetbaggers swarmed the region, doing their best to lift black men over good white men. But finally that nightmare came to an end. Order was re-established and white men took their rightful place in society. The peculiar institution was not revived, but an arrangement that insured the new prosperity of the planter class was begun; sharecropping.

The colonel had taken it upon himself to chase and bring back the group of Negroes who had conspired to cheat their landowner. Old man Timothy Burnsides had washed his hands of it; they weren't the first ones to slip off into the night and wouldn't be the last. But people like Burnsides couldn't see the implications. The more Negroes escaping to the West, the more that would do the same. Soon the South would be robbed of their labor which couldn't be replaced by coolies from the West.

His men finally reached the summit of the hill. Johnny Prescott and Marcus Peterson weren't the brightest men he knew, but they were loyal and followed orders. Both had served in his command during the war and both had hit on hard times afterwards. Wilson had done his best to provide for them, and this was another opportunity to do so. They had set out with twelve men, but only Prescott and Calhoun remained.

Prescott took off his hat then wiped away the sweat with a soiled handkerchief.

"Begging your pardon Colonel, but how much farther you suspect we have to chase these niggers?"

"We follow them until we apprehend them and bring them back to Mississippi," the colonel replied. "I shouldn't have to tell you this, Corporal."

He addressed the men referring to their former rank as they did him. It served to keep discipline.

"I don't know, Colonel," Peterson worried. "I think the others had the right idea. The hell with them. Let 'em go. They'll probably starve anyway. What they going to do without a white man telling them what to do?"

The colonel sat up in his saddle, which seemed to make Prescott and Calhoun slump.

"Those other men with us were playing soldier," he said. "They aren't veterans like us. They're weak to the rigors of campaigning. You both know what we fought for. What we do now is an extension of that. It is essential that we capture these wayward Negroes and set an example for others of what will not be tolerated."

"War's over, Colonel," Peterson pointed out.

"The war is never over!"

The colonel reached into his saddle bag then took out a leather pouch. He threw the pouch at Peterson, striking him in the chest. Peterson caught it.

"There," Pickett sneered. "The rest of your pay. It's becoming more and more obvious to me why you never progressed beyond the rank of private. Go back to Mississippi. But remember this. If we keep turning away from every discretion, we'll soon find ourselves crushed under a black heel again and the next time it won't stop until we are one with the mud. Do you want that for you and your family, Calhoun?"

"I ain't got a family," Peterson replied. "But I get what you're saying. I'll stay on, but it's only three of us now. How we going to get a hundred folks to turn back around and follow us back to Mississippi when they sure as hell don't want to?"

"And they probably have guns," Prescott added. "Lots of them."

Both men spoke the truth.

"We'll need more men," the colonel said. He went into his saddlebag again, extracting a folded map. He opened the map then took a pencil from his coat.

"We're not far from a town called Felicity," he pointed to the map. "We should reach it in a few days if the weather stays as it is. Once we arrive we'll gather more riders."

"Begging your pardon once again sir," Prescott said. "These folks probably ain't going want to risk their lives for our cause."

"I have gold," the colonel reminded them. "It's a language they'll understand. We'll gather as many as we can."

"Well if you don't mind, Colonel, I think I'll keep my portion. Just in case."

"Do what you wish, Peterson. That's enough discussion. We have miles to make up."

The trio headed down the slope, the colonel frowning along the way. Peterson wasn't the only veteran that had lost the fervor of the Cause. Soon there would be few men like him remaining. But that was in the future. For now, he would continue to serve. He cleared his mind and focused on the journey ahead.

Katy rode into Felicity slumped in her saddle and covered with trail dust. The ride to the quiet town had been more arduous than normal due to the drought hanging over the valley like a buzzard over a ripe carcass. She wasn't much on towns or cities, preferring her solitude, but the lack of good hunting and a weak harvest forced her into town to buy supplies and possibly find work. The latter was more dream than reality; few were willing to hire a woman for what was considered men's work, and fewer still a Negro woman.

She guided her horse down the ill-kept streets to the hitching post before the general store. As she walked toward the door she saw a sight almost as rare as her in town; a Negro man wearing a preacher's collar standing before the store counter. Billy Darden, the store owner, looked up at the tall man with an expression of disgust.

"Now look here boy," he said. "I done already told you I ain't got none of the supplies you're looking for!"

The man sighed. "Sir, I got a wagon train of one hundred people depending on me to bring those supplies back. Now I can clearly see that you have everything I need. I'm appealing to your Christian faith to help us out in this time of need. I got the gold right here. All I need is for you to treat us fair and square, that's all."

Billy took his shotgun from under the counter.

"Look boy, this is the last time I'm telling you. Get out of my store before they have to drag you out!"

The Negro preacher raised his hands.

"Ain't no need for violence, sir. I'll be moving on. God bless you."

Katy stepped to the side then turned her back as the preacher exited the

"Get out of my store before they have to drag you out!"

"Good doing business with you, Billy."

"Don't never come back here again."

"Oh, I'll be back," Katy stated coldly. "And you'll give me what I pay for. Otherwise little Mike here will be running this store."

Katy turned her back on Billy then went to her horse. She tied it to the wagon then climbed inside.

"Alright preacher man," she whispered. "Let's get you your supplies."

Katy pushed the mule hard. The preacher had a good head start and was riding with less weight. But Katy had a good idea where to find him and his wagon train. There were very few places along the north road where a group as big as the preacher described could camp, and without supplies they would have to scrounge the grasses for wild game. She cracked her whip and the mule bayed in protest.

"I ain't got no time for backtalk mule!" she shouted. "Get us where we need to be and you won't have to worry about Katy."

Katy and the mule crested the hill above Shamus Creek an hour before dusk. The preacher's wagon train was scattered on both sides of the shallow creek. The folks had cleared a spot near the creek and filled it with cooking fires. A man sitting on a roan stallion and sporting a Union jacket and cap spotted her first; he whistled then rode toward her. The others emerged from their wagons and gathered close to the fires. The man cradled a Sharps rifle against his chest, holding the reins in his right hand. A thick moustache drooped around his mouth. Katy smiled as his eyebrows rose.

"Well you're quite a sight," he said, his southern drawl thick like her parents. "The last thing I expected to see way out here was a Negro woman alone."

"Last thing I expected to see out here was a wagon train of Negroes," Katy returned. "My name is Katy Calhoun and I have something for the preacher."

The man tipped his hat. "Jason Jones. Folks call me Jay. Reverend Stills is in camp. You best follow me."

Jay and Katy entered the camp. The curious folks immediately surrounded the wagon, their expressions ranging from joyful to suspicious.

"Hey Reverend!" Jay yelled. "Someone's here to see you!"

The Reverend stuck his head out of a wagon near the fire, a puzzled look on his face. He climbed out of the wagon and was quickly followed by a petite light-skinned woman who glared at Katy suspiciously. Katy snickered as she climbed out of her wagon; looked like the Reverend was going to have some explaining to do.

store, dropping a piece of paper as he went to his horse. She noticed the revolver stuck in the front of his pants as well. He mounted then stared at the store.

"This place ain't no better than Mississippi," he commented. "Lord, how far we got to go to get away from this evil?"

He spurred his horse and galloped down the road. Katy picked up the paper; it was the list of supplies the preacher tried to buy. She strode into the store, removing her scarf to reveal her handsome face. Billy looked up then smiled.

"Well, well, if it ain't Katy Calhoun. What brings you to Felicity?"

"Crops went bad and game is scarce because of the drought. Wouldn't be here otherwise," Katy said. "Gonna need some supplies to get me through the winter."

"What do you need?"

Katy reached into her jacket and pulled her list. Billy studied the list and nodded.

"No problem," he said.

"I'll be needing this too…for a friend."

Katy placed the preacher's list on the counter. Billy looked at the list then scowled.

"Now wait just a god damn minute…"

Katy pulled back her jacket, revealing her ivory handled six-shooter.

"Billy, we've known each other for a long time. Now I can't say we're friends, but I'm sure we're not enemies. But we're going to be if you don't fill both of those orders. You know good and well what happens to my enemies."

Billy stomped back into the storage room, bringing the supplies and stacking them on the counter.

"I'm gonna need a mule and wagon, too," Katy added.

"Mike!" Billy shouted.

Mike Stanton, Billy's nephew, stuck his head into the door.

"Yeah, Uncle Billy?"

"Go around back and get Katy here a mule and wagon."

"Yes sir!"

The boy smiled at Katy. "Hiya Quickshot!" he greeted. "You sure look pretty today."

"Git on now boy!" Billy ordered.

Katy and Billy glared at each other as Mike brought the wagon around then loaded it with the supplies. Katy paid the full amount.

"Reverend, this young lady says she has something for you," Jay said with a smirk.

"I couldn't imagine what," the Reverend puzzled. "I've never seen her before in my life." Katy could tell the Reverend uttered those words more for his wife than for anything else.

"No Reverend, you never met me," Katy said. "I saw you back in Felicity trying to buy supplies. You walked right by me on your way out. You had good reason not to notice me."

She walked to the wagon and pulled back the canvas.

"I think this is what you went to town for."

The Reverend's eyes widened at the sight of the supplies.

"Everybody gather around!" He waved his arms. "The Lord has provided!"

The people rushed to the wagon then cheered. They immediately grabbed each other's hands, forming a human ring. Katy held the hand of the Reverend's wife on the right and Jay Jay's on the left. The Reverend stood in the middle of the circle.

"Let us bow our heads," he began. "Dear Lord, thank you for blessing us with this bounty. Our journey has been filled with trials and tribulations but you still have not abandoned your children. Once again you've sent one of your angels to watch over us. In the everlasting name of Jesus Christ, Amen."

"Amen," the others echoed.

Katy placed her hands on her hips.

"Now that's a first. I've never been called an angel before."

"But you are!" the reverend's wife said. "I'm Precious Stills, Reverend Stills' wife."

"Glad to meet you," Katy smiled. She pushed past Precious to the reverend.

"Those supplies cost me five dollars, preacher."

"Oh, of course!" the reverend replied. "Precious, please go to the wagon and bring five dollars for..."

"Katy. Katy Calhoun."

"Miss Calhoun," he finished.

Katy tipped her hat. "Much obliged to you."

"Thank you again, Miss Calhoun. It seems the evils of some people continue to follow us."

"Felicity ain't one of the friendliest towns in these parts," she concurred. "Especially when it comes to Negroes."

"Yet he sold the supplies to you?"

"I'm known around these parts. Besides, I can be very persuasive when I have to be."

Katy patted her guns. The reverend eyes widened.

"Lord Jesus, I hope you didn't kill anyone!"

Katy laughed. "Not this time."

The reverend frowned. "The taking of life is nothing to joke about."

Katy's smile faded. "I ain't joking."

Miss Stills' appearance broke the tense mood.

"Here you are ma'am," she said. "Five dollars."

Katy counted out the money then grinned.

"Looks like our business is done. I'll be getting along now."

"No, please stay and have supper with us," Miss Stills invited.

"Yes, please do," the reverend agreed. "It's almost dark and we'd love to have your company. Besides, if it wasn't for you supper would be a little sparse."

Jay walked up then stood beside her. "Yeah Katy, you should stay."

Jay had that sly smile on his face that men displayed when food was the last thing on their mind. Katy smiled back.

"All right, I think I will stay. No way will I make it back to town before dark, and I'm not too fond of sleeping by myself tonight."

Jay's smile widened. "That would be unsafe."

"Good!" Precious said. She grabbed Katy by the hand as she scowled at Jay.

"You can help us women prepare the meal."

"I'm not that good of a cook," Katy admitted.

"That's okay," Precious scoffed. "The rest of us will make up for your shortcomings. C'mon now."

Katy gave Jay an 'I'm sorry' glance then followed Precious and the other women to help prepare supper. She took the easiest task, peeling potatoes, while the others cut and chopped and seasoned the provisions she brought from the general store. Precious was in command, shouting orders to the other women while talking to Katy between shouts.

"It's not good for a young lady like you to be living alone in such a wild place," she opined.

"I'm doing all right," Katy replied. "Seem to remember I wasn't the one about to starve without food."

Precious cut a mean eye at Katy. "Still, you never know when a man might try to take advantage of your innocence."

"You don't know who you're talking to," Katy said. "I ain't one of your church girls. I've been living in this territory for over ten years and ain't no man every got nothing from me unless I wanted to give it. And those who tried are keeping company with the Devil in Hell."

Katy patted her side arm. The other ladies laughed; Precious glared at them and they fell silent.

"You talk as bad as the men folk," Precious declared.

"Sometimes I'm as bad as them," Katy countered. "Look Mrs. Stills, I appreciate your concern, but my mama died a long time ago and I ain't looking for another one. How about you staying out of my business and let's enjoy this good supper y'all ladies are preparing. Besides, Jay ain't my type. Too bowlegged. Man looks like he had rickets or something."

Precious didn't have too much to say to Katy after their conversation. The supper was delicious; Katy never could have imagined so much being done with so little. After dinner she sat at the fire, captivating the wagon train folks with stories of growing up in the Oklahoma Territory. She spent the night sleeping by the Reverend's wagon, much to Jay's disappointment. She wasn't lying when she told Precious Jay wasn't her type. That never stopped her before from taking a man for a roll, but being in the camp with so many religious folks dampened any desire she might have had for the ex-Union soldier.

She was up with the daylight, inspecting the wagon before her ride back to town.

"Leaving so early?" the reverend asked.

"Yes sir. Got to get this wagon back and get on my way. Thank you kindly for supper last night. I'll be praying that you and your people get to your land without any more trouble."

Katy was climbing into the wagon as Jay rode up.

"I can follow you a ways to make sure you're safe," he offered.

Katy laughed. "I've been safe all this time before I met you. I think I'll be alright. You look out for them folks, okay?"

Jay tipped his hat with a smile.

"I'll be seeing you, Katy Calhoun," he said.

Katy gave him a knowing smile.

"You sure will."

Colonel Pickett was not impressed with Felicity. He was hoping for a larger town but the collection of buildings was the largest settlement within twenty miles, so it would have to do. There was no local sheriff according to the townsfolk. Law and order was administered by a visiting judge and US marshal, a man named Bass Reeves. The townsfolk described him as a Negro, which brought a bitter taste to Pickett's mouth. The idea of a black man presiding over good and honest white people went against everything he stood for. If he had the time he would wait until this Reeves man passed through and show him a bit of Southern justice. Unfortunately he had a job to do and a home to return to. He wasn't here to make Oklahoma Mississippi.

The trio walked into the saloon. Pickett stood at the swing door and studied the establishment while the corporal and private made their way to the bar. The Colonel never let the sin of liquor pass through his lips. Alcohol dulled the senses, and for a man like him he had to be vigilant if not for himself for the sake of others. His men were on their second drink by the time he reached the bar. He took off his riding gloves and extended his hand to the barkeep.

"Hello sir," he began. "I'm Colonel Wilson Pickett. These are my men, Corporal John Prescott and Private Marcus Peterson."

The barkeep took his hand with a slight grip then shook it.

"Kyle Swan," he said. "You know the war's over, right?"

The Colonel scowled as Peterson chuckled.

"I'm aware of that, Mr. Swan."

"Just checking," Swan said. "We get a few loco hombres in here from time to time. What are you having?"

"I don't drink," the colonel replied. "I'll get to the point. I'm looking for good men to assist us in apprehending a group of Negro fugitives fleeing Mississippi. We've been tasked to capture them and take them back to stand trial."

Kyle looked the men over.

"I've heard you mention rank, but I don't see no badges. This ain't the South, and a few folks out here fought on the other side. They might not take kindly to the three of y'all out here sniffing about for colored folks."

"Just answer my question, Mr. Swan," the colonel ordered.

Prescott and Peterson had put down their drinks and were staring at the barkeep. Swan raised his hands.

"I ain't looking for trouble. Just expressing my opinion and sharing a few words of warning. There may be a few around here that would join your posse for the right price."

"And where would I find these men?"

"Come back around dusk. The shops will be closeed and a few of the farmhands will be here for a few drinks and poker."

"Excellent," the colonel approved. "In the meantime we need lodging. Is there a hotel available?"

"No hotel, but Miss Laney down the road rents rooms and cooks a good meal. Just sent a fellow down her way yesterday."

The colonel tipped his hat. "Much obliged to you sir. Peterson, Prescott; finish your drinks. We need to be on our way."

The two men downed their shots then followed the colonel to the saloon entrance.

"Enjoy your stay, Johnny Reb," Kyle called out.

The three men looked at the barkeep and he winked.

"Like I said, a few of us fought on the winning side."

The colonel gave him a curt nod then stormed out the saloon, his men trailing behind him.

Katy took her time getting the wagon back to Felicity. She had enjoyed her time with the wagon train despite Mrs. Stills lecturing. It had been some time since she had spent time with friendly folks and it felt good to be able to sleep without one eye open for trouble. She wished them better luck than most settlers that had come to the territory; she had a feeling that these folks would make it work. Unlike the others, they had nothing to go back to.

By the time she reached town the sun was setting. As she took the wagon around back she noticed a large number of horses hitched in front of the saloon. Some were familiar; others were definitely from out of town. Mike Stanton was sitting behind the store whittling when Katy arrived. He jumped to his feet, dropping the wood then folding his knife and shoving it into his pocket.

"Howdy Miss Katy!" he waved.

"Hi Mike." Katy climbed down from the wagon. "You take good care of my ponies?"

Mike poked out his chest as he grasped his suspenders. "Yes ma'am!"

Katy took a silver dollar out of her pocket then flipped to the boy. Mike snatched it out of the air, a wide grin on his freckled face.

"Thank you, Miss Katy!"

Katy motioned her head toward the saloon. "What's going on in there?"

"Three men rode in from Mississippi yesterday," Mike said. "Say they're looking for some nig...I mean Negroes that stole some property from them. They're gathering up a posse to go after them."

Katy felt a surge of anger. She reached into her pocket and pulled out another silver dollar.

"I'll give you another one of these if you'll go inside and unlatch the back door."

"You got it, Miss Katy!"

Katy tossed Mike another coin. He caught it, shoved it in his pocket, grabbed his hat then sprinted to the saloon. Katy took a more leisurely pace, making sure no one was looking when she slipped into the alley between the saloon and the livery then trotted to the rear of the building. She waited until the door opened. Mike stuck out his head and smiled. Katy ran to the door.

"You go on now, Mike, and keep quiet about this."

"I will ma'am."

Katy followed Mike to the saloon's bar area. He walked through the door but didn't close it all the way. Katy peeked inside. The saloon was filled with men; a few of them wanted criminals. Standing before the bar were three men dressed Eastern style, one with an expensive felt hat on his head. The bartender leaned on the bar, listening to the men as well. It looked as though the meeting was about to commence. Katy settled into her hiding place and listened.

"I thank you for giving me a bit of your time," the man said with a heavy Southern drawl. "I'm...Wilson Pickett, and these are my companions, John Prescott and Marcus Peterson. A few weeks ago we set out from Mississippi in pursuit of a group of Negroes posing as homesteaders. These Negroes purchased land with money stolen from their landlord and plan on settling on it. They are being led by a Negro man named Percival Stills, a charlatan posing as a man of faith. Since our pursuit of these lawbreakers our numbers have diminished, so I am seeking those willing to help us apprehend the perpetrators. Since the money used to purchase the land was stolen from my employer, he had authorized me to offer a plot of land to anyone that wishes to be compensated as such, up to the limit available."

One of the listeners spoke up. "I've been wanting to take up farming myself. I guess this would be a right time to do it. I'm in."

Another man joined in. "I ain't interested in no farm. Give me the money and I'll be fine. Been a while since I've been coon hunting."

A round of laughter spread through the room.

Katy recognized the man interested in the money. It was the talker, the man who escaped her. Her hand went to her revolver but she took it away.

"Not here," she whispered. "Not yet."

"That's two," Pickett said. "Are there anymore volunteers?"

Leroy Barnes, a rotund man with a thick beard and wide eyes stepped forward.

"You boys fought in the war," he said. "On the rebel side."

Wilson didn't reply. His men stood straight, hands falling to their sides.

"Yes we did," Pickett said.

Leroy spit on the floor the marched out the saloon.

"That was unfortunate," Pickett continued. "We all have a past, but as your barkeep reminded me earlier, the war is over. Now, is anyone else interested in bringing these Negroes to justice?"

A scattering of hands rose while others followed Barnes out the door. Prescott counted the raised hands.

"That makes fifteen. That's all we can afford."

Another man stepped forward, a thin man wearing worn overalls and a straw hat.

"Which way these folks headed?" he asked.

"What's your name, sir?" Pickett inquired.

"Bill Hawthorne. I got a farm about a mile south of town. If they're heading west to unclaimed land, they'll have to cross Cold River at the ford. That's as good a place as any to set a trap."

Others in the room nodded in agreement. Katy did as well.

"Thanks for nothing, Hawthorne," she whispered.

"That's excellent information Mr. Hawthorne," Pickett smiled cruelly. "Gentlemen we have our posse. Meet us in front of the saloon in three days. We'll ride to Cold River ford like Billy here suggested and set up the ambush."

Katy had heard enough. She hurried out the back of the saloon. To her pleasant surprise Mike was waiting with her ponies.

"I figured you'd be needing these," he said.

Katy scrambled onto her roan mare. She tossed Mike another dollar.

"I hope you can help them folks," the boy added. "They ain't done nothing to nobody."

"I damn sure plan to," Katy vowed. "Even if I have to die trying. But first I'm gonna need some help, and I know just where to find it."

She spurred her horse then galloped out of town. Katy rode hard, stopping only at sundown. She was up early the next morning, keeping a hard pace until she saw the wagon train in the distance. She switched to a fresh horse and left the other behind as she galloped ahead. The wagon train folks smiled and waved at her as she rode to the lead wagon. Reverend Stills and Precious sat on the buckboard of their Conestoga; Jason rode his horse leading the way, his Sharps rifle lying across his saddle. They smiled when they recognized her.

"Miss Calhoun!" the reverend said. "So you've decided to join us after all."

"Not exactly, Reverend. I've come to bring you some bad news."

The smiles faded from their faces. Jason guided his horse closer to Katy.

"Them folks you left in Mississippi are here, and they're looking for you," Katy reported.

"Oh my Lord!" Precious exclaimed. The reverend patted his wife on the shoulder. "Don't fret, Precious. We're in the hand of the Almighty."

"I don't know about the Lord's hands, but you're sure enough in mine," Katy advised. "You're going to have to get off this trail. It'll lead you right to the ambush they're planning to set up."

"We can't do that," Jason argued. "The best place to ford Cold River is the way we're headed."

"You ain't fording the river, not any time soon." Katy tipped back her hat then leaned forward on her saddle horn.

"Reverend, you're going to ride up to the next clearing then make camp. Don't leave that place until me and Jason return."

Jason looked puzzled. "Return? Where are we going?"

Katy grinned. "We're going to ruin a surprise. But we have a stop to make first."

"What stop?"

"The two of us ain't enough," Katy said. "I'm sure of what I can do, but I'm not sure about you. No offense."

"None taken," the ex-soldier said.

"We need one more person, and I know exactly where he is."

"How do you now he'll help?"

"He'll help alright. This is what he was born to do."

B ass Reeves swung the axe downward, splitting the wood with one stroke. Chopping wood was the order of the day. It would be winter soon and there was never enough. He took the split lumber then added it to the growing stack then balanced another piece on the chopping block. He was raising his axe when he spied two riders approaching. He dropped

"Miss Calhoun! So you've decided to join us after all."

his axe then strolled to the front porch of his modest home, picking up the Winchester propped against the side of the house. As the most successful US marshal in the Oklahoma Territory he was bound to have enemies hunting him down. As the riders neared a grin lifted his wide moustache.

"I'll be damned," he said to himself. "Quickshot Katy."

He relaxed a bit but not completely. He didn't recognize the man riding with Katy, so it was best to retain a little wariness. Katy was a petty criminal at the least, a vigilante at the most. A few local lawmen might have an issue with her but there was nothing she'd ever done that would put her on the wrong side of the U.S. law. He'd known her parents, escaped slaves just like him hiding in the untamed territory. He watched her grow up into the woman she was, though he had to admit he was a bit disappointed how she turned out. A hard life in a hard land can twist a person in different ways.

When her face came into full view Bass could tell there was something amiss. He stood straight then tipped his hat.

"Katy Calhoun," he smiled. "What brings you to my doorstep?"

"I need your help Bass," she answered. "Got a wagon train of Negroes from Mississippi about to be ambushed by a posse claiming they're thieves."

"Maybe they are," Bass replied.

"No they ain't sir," the man with the union cap said.

"And who might you be?" Bass questioned.

"Jason Jones, formerly of the 54th Massachusetts. Sharpshooter."

"That don't mean nothing to me," Bass replied.

"I ain't got no time for your suspicions," Katy interjected. "If we don't ride out right now these folks are going to die. You know my word is good. Besides, there are a couple of boys riding with that posse that you got warrants on. So are you coming or ain't you?"

"Give me a minute, girl."

Bass went inside his house to gather the tools of his trade. He strapped on his sidearms then packed a change of clothes, ammunition and provisions into two saddlebags. He locked up the house then ambled to the barn for his horses. Chopping wood would have to wait. He mounted his mare then wrapped the reins of his stallion around his shoehorn. Ready to travel, he rode his horse up to Katy.

"Where're we headed?"

"The ford at Cold River."

"A good place for an ambush," Bass said.

Katy grinned. "Yes it is."

Bass frowned. "Now Katy, if there are fugitives in the posse like you said I need to take them alive. You know I ain't for no unnecessary killing."

"You ain't got to worry about me as long as you handle your business properly," Katy explained her reasoning. "That's why I came to fetch you. I figure the sight of a little law and order would make them back down. But if they start shooting I'm gonna shoot back, and you know I don't often miss."

"Neither do I," Jason chimed in.

Bass shook his head. "Fair enough. Let's ride."

The trio pushed hard through the Oklahoma landscape, finally arriving at the Cold River ford at dusk. As Katy said it was the perfect place for an ambush. This section of the river ran through a shallow valley bordered by wooded hills. The road leading to the ford was wooded as well, providing shade for a wagon train, or in this case, a hiding place for those of ill intent. Bass raised his hand as they reached the summit of the hill overlooking the river.

"We'll camp out here," he directed. "No fire. We'll let that posse move in and set up before we move in."

"They'll set their own trap and we'll bag' em," Katy assumed.

"Not exactly," Bass corrected.

"What are you talking about?" Jason asked. He looked at Katy, "What is he talking about?"

"As a US marshal I'm required to give a man a chance to surrender before attempting to arrest him by force," Bass explained.

"Ain't no such damn thing," Katy snapped. "Wanted dead or alive. That's what the posters say."

"I want them alive," Bass held his ground. "If you want my help, that's the way it's got to be."

Jason rode up to Bass. His face was not pleasant.

"Mister, did you fight in the war?"

"I was a slave," Bass related. "Went to the war to serve my master. One day we got into a disagreement over a card game and I whipped him good. Been wanting to do it for quite some time. Of course after that I had to run. That's how I ended up in Oklahoma."

Jason's mood seemed to calm a bit after Bass's words.

"Then you know what kind of folks we're dealing with, Marshal. Every time I marched into battle I knew them damn graybacks was either going to kill me on the spot or send me back to slavery so I fought like a wildcat. I didn't ask for no quarter and I didn't give it. The three men coming after these folks were all graybacks. Hell, the leader was an officer. Going to be hard for me not to put a bullet in them."

"As far as we know they ain't broke no laws," Bass said. "If they cooperate we let them be and send them on their way. If they don't, then you'll get your chance."

Jason nodded. "Fair enough."

They rode their horses to the spot Bass chose then set up camp. Katy rolled out her blanket in a soft spot then went immediately asleep. Bass stretched out as well, pulling his hat down over his eyes to get a bit of rest himself.

"How'd you become a US marshal?" Jason asked.

Bass frowned. Seemed he wouldn't get much rest after all.

"After I escaped I fell in with the local Indians," he began. "They taught me how to shoot, track and live off the land. Learned this land like the back of my hand. Oklahoma was wild back then. A lot of lawbreakers and deserters would come and lay low on the account that the government didn't have jurisdiction here."

"Shoot, it's wild now," Jason chuckled.

"You ain't seen nothing, boy," Bass went on. "Because I knew the land so well the marshals would come by my house to help them find whoever was hiding out. After a while they decided to kill two birds with one stone. They asked me if I wanted to be a marshal. The pay was good and the work was steady so I said yes."

Bass lifted his head high enough to see Jason's serious face.

"How about you? Why did you decide to come out this way?"

Jason pulled a grass stalk then chewed on it.

"Wasn't no way I was gonna stay down South after the Federal troops left. I escaped with Moses before the war. When it finally broke out I was eager to fight. Had family I wanted to see free and I always felt bad leaving them. It was a joyful day when they finally let us Negroes fight."

Jason took the stalk from his lips. "I ain't known war was gonna be like it was. I saw some things a man wasn't supposed to see. I still see them sometimes. Lots of boys run off, black and white. But I promised to see it through and I did."

"You find your family?" The lawman asked.

"Most of them. Some of them had already run off before the war was over. If they were smart they went up North or they came out here. I was one of them stupid enough to stay South. I thought things were going to be better and they were for a time. But then the soldiers left and the Klan started riding and it was Hell all over again. But like the last time I wasn't taking it. When the reverend came to me to lead his people out here he saved my life. I was about to be lynched any minute."

Bass sat up, leaning on his right arm. "Why was that?"

Jason lifted his Sharps. "Like I said, I wasn't taking it."

A grin came to Bass's face as he eased back down to his blanket and closed his eyes.

"Got to admire a man who fights for what he believes in. You better get some rest. I suspect that despite my best efforts you'll have some more fighting to do."

Jason nodded. "I suspect I will."

"I'll take first watch," Bass volunteered.

Jason laid out his blanket then fell asleep. Bass leaned against the nearest tree then settled in for his watch. He glanced over at Jason and Katy, sadness creeping into his thoughts. Life was hard enough without having to deal with what Negroes had to go through. But things weren't going to change any time soon. He let that brief moment of pity pass. He was a US marshal and he had work to do.

Katy touched him on the shoulder and relieved him on watch. He went off and slept hard as he was prone to do when on a hunt. He was awakened by Jason's serious face.

"They're coming," the sharpshooter whispered.

Bass jumped up from the blanket and followed Jason to where Katy crouched. She looked at the two of them then grinned.

"Looks like they picked up a few folks along the way," she said. "I count at least 30 of them."

Bass looked at the riders approaching and a bitter taste invaded his mouth.

"Half of them are just here to watch," he surmised.

"They think it's going to be a lynching," Jason stated the obvious.

Jason lay on the ground and positioned his Sharps. Bass put his hand on the barrel.

"We had an agreement," he reminded the marksman.

"It's thirty of them," Katy pointed out. "I say we trim the herd before we start negotiating."

Bass strolled to his horse. "I'm riding ahead. I'll meet them before they cross the river. You two get yourselves in position behind them. And no shooting until I say so."

Bass climbed onto his horse then rode off before Katy or Jason could protest. He worked his way down the hills then onto the trail well ahead of the posse. He coaxed his horses into the shallow river to the opposite bank then waited. A half an hour later the first riders of the posse crested the hill. Bass figured their initial intentions would be to fan out into the brush to set the ambush. However, they picked up the pace toward the river. They'd seen him. By the time they reached the opposite bank the ringleaders had separated themselves from the group. Another man rode with them, a man whose face Bass knew well.

One of the men, a red-faced fellow with a wide brim hat and bristling mustache rode forward, accompanied by the fugitive Tom Bowden. Bowden had a one hundred dollar bounty on his head and was as slippery as a greased fish. He tipped his hat back and grinned.

"I knew it," he said. "Bass Reeves."

"Hello, Marshal Reeves," the other man said. "I'm Colonel Wilson Pickett. To what do I owe this meeting?"

Bass nodded. "Colonel Pickett, it has come to my attention that you plan on apprehending a group of settlers bound for land which they purchased. It has also come to my attention that your posse contains a number of men that are wanted for various crimes against the federal government. As a U.S. marshal, I'll have to ask you to abandon your pursuit of these innocent people and turn over the fugitives within your group."

The colonel smirked. "Marshal, those people that you claim to be innocent stole from me. The wagons and tools in their possession are items that were loaned to them in order to farm the property I owned under the sharecropping agreements that they signed. In my book that constitutes stealing."

"If you're accusing these folks of theft then this is an issue that should be settled in a court of law, not with an armed posse," Bass replied. "And by the looks of your group, I get the feeling you're not interested in due process."

The colonel's face shifted into a hard façade.

"Look boy, I don't care if some damn fool decided to pin a badge on your chest. These damn folks stole from their landlord and broke their contracts. I'm taking every last one of them back to Mississippi. Those that resist can stay here…in their graves."

Bowden laughed. "That's right, nigger. Now get the hell out of here."

Bass lowered his head then shook it. "I'm sorry you feel that way."

When he looked up he had his revolvers in his hands.

"You're under arrest. All of you."

The colonel and Bowden laughed.

"You actually think you're going to arrest us all by yourself?"

Bass grinned. "Who said I was by myself?"

"The hell with this!" Bowden exclaimed. He went for his gun. Bowden was fast but Bass was faster. He shot the fugitive in the arm. No sooner did a bullet graze Bass's shoulder, knocking him backwards. The colonel turned then galloped away; Bass heard the report of a Sharps rifle and the colonel tumbled from his horse. Bedlam ensued; the posse began shooting in every direction while being cut down by Jason's deadly fire. Those who came as spectators fled down the road back to Felicity, yelling and screaming along the way. Bass waded across the river, shooting with both his firearms. As he reached the back he saw Katy emerge from the brush, firing her Winchester from the waist. More posse members fell and jumped from their horses seeking cover as she worked her way closer to the group. Some were able to find cover and began shooting back, forcing Katy to find cover herself.

Bass aimed at Katy then fired. Her hat flew off her head; she turned in his direction, her Winchester at her shoulder. Bass motioned to the right with his head then sprinted in the same direction as Katy laid down cover fire. She was soon joined by Jay, the distinct sound of his Sharps rifle echoing between the hills. Bass sneaked until he was behind the posse members, their attention drawn to Katy and Jay. Once he was in position he began shooting. He could have easily killed at least half of them, but that wasn't his way. Instead he shot to miss, forcing the posse to make a hard choice. They were caught in a crossfire. A smart leader would have split forces, half taking on Katy and Jay and other half dealing with Bass. But Colonel Pickett was wounded and the other men were just farmers and bandits trying to make easy money. They never expected a gunfight. So they did what desperate and afraid men do. They surrendered.

The three converged on the posse. Bass spied the other fugitives; Billy Wainwright and Will Gunderson.

"Everyone drop your guns!" Bass shouted. Most of the posse complied; a few held onto them, their looks defiant.

Katy raised her rifle. "Drop' em now or I start back shooting."

"Me, too," Jason said.

The others dropped their weapons.

"You two," Bass pointed to the fugitives. "Come on out."

The men trudged up to Bass. He whistled and his horse trotted to his side. Bass took rope from his saddlebag then tied the men to their horses He climbed onto his horse before speaking to the others.

"The rest of you get out here. If I ever see any of you on the wrong of the side of the law again I'll make sure you spend the rest of your life in federal prison. Understand?"

The other men nodded. Bass looked at Katy and Jason.

"Let them go."

"Are you serious?" Jason queried.

"Yes. Let them go."

Jason spit before lowering his rifle. The men ran to their horses then galloped away over the rise, all except the riders from Mississippi. They rode to the body of the colonel then loaded him onto his horse. They took their time sharing a dangerous look with the trio.

"This ain't over," one of them yelled.

Katy cocked her Winchester. "It can be. Right now."

Bass maneuvered his horse between Katy and the Mississippi men.

"Back down, Katy. You shoot those men I'll have to take you in, too."

"I don't let folks that threaten my life live."

"Girl, I said simmer down."

Katy lowered her rifle slightly.

"I'll give you a head start," she compromised.

The men rode off as fast as their horses allowed. Katy laughed as she rested her rifle on her shoulder.

"I thought I was going to have to take you down," Bass said.

"You couldn't have if you wanted to. Jason wouldn't have let you."

"No I wouldn't have," Jason affirmed.

Bass shook his head as he grinned.

"You two ain't the best help I ever had, but you were good enough."

He focused his attention on Katy.

"You can't go back to Felicity. You know that, right?"

Katy shrugged. "It was never my home anyway. Folks there just tolerated me. Everybody except that boy Michael Stanton. Poor kid is sweet on me."

Bass watched as Katy strolled into the bush then return on her horse.

"I reckon I'll hook up with the reverend and his people for a while until things cool down," Katy voiced her thoughts. "They could use an extra gun, and Jason could use some company. Ain't that right, Jason?"

Jason grinned like a gambler on a winning streak. "That's right, Katy."

"You two best get on then, and tell the reverend I wish him good luck," Bass said.

"What you going to do with them two?" Jason asked.

"We ain't far from Pembroke," Bass answered. "Sheriff Coleman and I are good friends. I'll have these fellows locked up by nightfall."

"Thank you, Bass," Katy added. "You done good for some good people."

"Only because you asked. Your folks done good raising you. You turned out okay after all."

"Don't let anybody hear you say that," Katy cautioned. "I have a reputation to uphold."

She tipped her hat to Bass then winked at Jason.

"Come on soldier boy. If we hurry we can catch up with the others before nightfall."

"I'm with you, Miz Katy."

Katy nodded. "I know you are."

Bass watched them ride off down trail as he shook his head.

"Young folks," he said aloud.

He looked at the fugitives and his smile faded.

"Let's get you boys to justice."

He kicked his mount and the three of them crossed Cold River on their way to Pembroke and justice.

THE END

The Black Wild West

I loved Westerns as a child. I watched the movies on Sunday in my hometown, and I was a big fan of The Rifleman, still one of my favorite television shows. But as a young black boy growing up in the sixties and in the South, I accepted the fact that there were no black people 'out West.' Of course I knew that wasn't literally true; my Aunt Lou moved with her husband to Monterrey and bore nine children. So I knew at least eleven black people out West. But to my knowledge no black people participated in the 'taming of the west.'

But then I grew older and more educated. I learned that black people had always been involved in the West, that many of the first 'cowboys' were black and Native American, and that stories of the West included people such as Nat Love, the Buffalo Soldiers and Stagecoach Mary. But it was only recently that I learned the story of arguably the greatest hero of the West, Bass Reeves. Bass Reeves is an icon for those who know him, a man who escaped slavery to survive in the Oklahoma Territory and grow to become one of the greatest US Marshals in history. As soon as I heard of Bass I knew I would write about him one day. This was another black historical figure whose story deserved to be told.

An opportunity presented itself earlier than I expected. Ron Fortier, another admirer of Bass Reeves, released a collection of fiction stories based on Bass Reeves life which I picked up immediately and enjoyed immensely. My enjoyment reached another level when Ron asked me to contribute a story to the second Bass Reeves anthology, which I happily obliged.

Stories about Bass Reeves are important to all Americans. For African Americans they highlight our contribution to the growth of this nation despite the burden of racism and discrimination that has plagued us to this day. His story and the story of other Black women and men that have made contributions to this country show black people, especially young black people, that they can achieve and contribute. It through fiction that most of us are introduced to history, and I hope that more people are

45

encouraged to learn more about Bass Reeves and the black participation in the West and the country through stories such as Ambush at Cold River and the other fine stories in this anthology.

MILTON DAVIS - is owner of MVmedia, LLC , a micro publishing company specializing in Science Fiction, Fantasy and Sword and Soul. MVmedia's mission is to provide speculative fiction books that represent people of color in a positive manner. Milton is the author of ten novels; his most recent is the Steamfunk adventure From Here to Timbuktu. He is the editor and co-editor of seven anthologies; *The City, Dark Universe* with Gene Peterson; *Griots: A Sword and Soul Anthology and Griot: Sisters of the Spear*, with Charles R. Saunders; *The Ki Khanga Anthology* , the *Steamfunk! Anthology*, and the Dieselfunk anthology with Balogun Ojetade. MVmedia has also published *Once Upon A Time in Afrika* by Balogun Ojetade and *Abegoni: First Calling* by Sword and Soul creator and icon Charles R. Saunders.

Milton resides in Metro Atlanta with his wife Vickie and his children Brandon and Alana.

TRAIN ROBBERY

By Mel Odom

"**I**f you don't wake up, you're going to miss the robbery."

The calm, quiet words, accompanied by a sharp elbow in the ribs, woke United States Deputy Marshal Bass Reeves. It took him a moment to digest what he'd been told. His seat juddered as the train rolled over the tracks.

The ride from the Indian Territories to Judge Isaac Parker's courtroom was supposed to be calm and provide Bass a chance to catch up on much needed rest. For the last few days, he'd been testifying in court and handling prisoners awaiting sentencing.

Blinking against the bright morning sunlight slanting through the passenger car's windows, he pushed his hat back and glanced to his left at Alfred Tubby, his posseman.

"What robbery?" Bass asked.

"The one we're having." Alfred nodded toward the front of the passenger car where two men aimed Winchester rifles at frightened passengers. Neckerchiefs covered the men's lower faces.

In his early seventies, twenty years older than Bass, Alfred sat quietly in his seat next to the deputy marshal. He was mostly Cherokee with some white thrown in by an unwelcome ancestor a few generations back. Scars from old violence marked his dark face here and there, and even though they'd ridden together off and on for years, Bass didn't know all of the stories that accompanied those scars. Alfred's long salt and pepper hair trailed down his back in a neat braid. Clad in boots, jeans, and a button-up shirt under a suit coat, he looked like just another Indian businessman riding the Katy line.

The two men brandishing Winchester rifles at the front of the train car appeared roughshod. Trail dust covered their worn clothing and chaps. They looked young and nervous, which was always a bad combination. The only thing that could have made it worse was liquor.

"I'm thinking maybe you coulda woke me up a little earlier," Bass said, "it being a train robbery and all."

47

Alfred smiled. "I didn't want to wake you for no reason. I didn't know that they were serious at first."

Bass glanced around the car. "There only two of them?"

"I'm betting there's at least one more. They have to have somebody on the engineers. That's how I would do it."

"You thought much about robbing trains?"

"It's something new to think about, inspired by recent events."

Ignoring the jibe, Bass worried about the people around them. A professional outlaw knew what he was doing, but these men didn't look professional. At least, they didn't seem at ease robbing the train. They were stiff and moved in a jerky fashion.

However, Bass had to admit that they looked downright determined because they didn't hesitate about pointing the guns and barking orders.

He wished he was armed, but he'd put his guns in the baggage car. Civilized men didn't ride heeled among civilized folks. Not even in the Territories.

Alfred shifted anxiously.

"Are you all right?" Bass asked.

Eyes bright, Alfred nodded and watched the gunmen eagerly. "I'm fine. I have to admit, though, I'm excited."

"You're *excited*?"

"It's my first train robbery."

"If you ask me, these things aren't all that exciting." Bass's stomach clenched a little.

"Lots of people have been on board when trains got robbed," Alfred said. "After it was over, they talk about how thrilled they got by the whole experience. I'm telling you, these railroad people need to think about putting on fake train robberies to liven things up during the long, dull stretches."

"All right, folks," the train robber in the front announced in a deep voice as he shifted his Winchester around the front rows, "ain't none of you gonna get hurt unless you act stupid. We're here for the payroll the train's carryin'."

"Of course," the other robber said, "that don't mean we ain't gonna be takin' nothin' from y'all." His mask couldn't hide the wide, frog-like grin under the material. He pulled a canvas bag from his coat pocket and shook it out till it opened the length of his arm. "We need one of y'all to volunteer to take up charitable donations."

No one moved or said a thing. The train thundered along the tracks without slackening pace.

"Cut one out of the herd," the first robber suggested. "Anybody ain't feelin' helpful, or feelin' charitable, is gonna catch a bullet this morning."

The second robber stepped toward the front row. As he got closer, Bass spotted the smallpox scars that dotted the man's forehead.

Breathing easy, watching as the pock-faced man gestured to one of the men sitting on the front row, Bass mentally flicked through images of the wanted posters he had memorized.

Leaning over to Alfred, not taking his eyes off the robbers, Bass said, "Does that look like Lloyd Fahrenthold? Got them pits in his face?"

The posseman paused in thought for a minute and his forehead creased. During that time, the pock-faced man dragged the "volunteer" to his feet and shoved the bag into the man's trembling hands.

"Now get out there an' do me proud," Pock-Face growled. With a big hand, he shoved the man toward the center of the passenger car. "Fill that bag with everythin' you can get. Cash. Watches. Gold teeth. We're takin' it all."

"That man's left little finger is missing," Alfred said. "Fahrenthold is missing a finger on his left hand."

"Who does he partner with? I know he used to ride with Ronnie Tatham, but Tatham got gunned down in a poker game in Durant a couple years ago."

"Maybe you could ask him to introduce you."

The Indian man in the banker's suit walked through the crowd with the bag open before him. He apologized to everyone who dropped cash and other valuables into the sack.

Fahrenthold followed closely behind and darted in to occasionally snatch a necklace or a bracelet from women who tried to hide their possessions.

Bass wondered if he stood a chance of making a break back for the baggage car and his weapons. Manhunting in the Territories could be confusing and troublesome. Some places tended to be civilized, but pockets of outlawry existed throughout the region. Generally speaking, folks who rode the trains like the Missouri-Kansas-Texas he was riding, were peaceable and law-abiding, and he respected their unspoken need to feel safe. When he rode the trains, he often didn't wear his guns. Most people frowned on a public display of weapons even from a member of the law.

"Jelly Eddie," Alfred said. "That's who the other man is. If you get a good look, you can see that knife scar just above the neckerchief on his right jaw. And he's missing the lower half of his ear."

Bass placed the name in a heartbeat. Jelly Eddie was actually Myron Eddie, a one-time railroad worker from California who'd turned bank robber. He was called "Jelly" because he specialized in using gelignite, a powerful explosive that was unstable in the hands of amateurs.

He leaned over to whisper to Alfred.

"Hey you." Eddie swiveled slightly and pointed his rifle at Bass.

Bass relaxed his face and looked innocent.

"What are you two whispering about back there?"

"The old man don't speak English," Bass said, changing his natural baritone to a higher-pitch out of reflex. He changed his dialect to a more backwoods version as well. Hiding in plain sight was one of his best skills. "I was tellin' him what you boys was sayin'."

"That right, old man? You don't understand what I'm sayin'?"

Alfred just sat there.

Nearby in the aisle, Fahrenthold stepped forward and raised his voice. *"You don't understand him, old man?"*

For a minute Bass worried that the outlaw might shoot Alfred.

"He said the old man don't know English," Eddie said. "Not that he was deaf, you idjit."

Fahrenthold's face warmed to scarlet around the pockmarks, which stayed white. "You don't have to call me names."

"My mistake," Eddie replied agreeably. "Just get 'em robbed an' let's be about our business. We got places to be an' the clock's tickin'."

Taking a fresh grip on his rifle, Fahrenthold stared at Bass. "Tell him to empty his pockets."

Speaking Cherokee, Bass "translated."

With a sour look, Alfred turned out his pockets, producing some coins and a few paper dollars that he thrust at the passenger turned bagman.

"I speak better English than you do," Alfred replied in Cherokee, "as well as better Cherokee."

"What's he sayin'?" Fahrenthold demanded of Bass.

"That he don't like givin' up his money," Bass answered.

Fahrenthold grinned as the bagman took Alfred's bills and the coins. "Now let's see what you got, big man."

Reluctantly, Bass turned out his pockets too, except for his inside jacket pocket. The small jewelry case inside was a surprise for his wife, Nellie. Bass dropped paper currency and coins into the bag, added his pocket watch and chain without being told because Fahrenthold had glanced at them.

"An' I'll have whatever you got inside your jacket pocket, too." Fahrenthold motioned with the rifle barrel, pointing at Bass's chest.

"That's just my makin's," Bass said, feeling stubborn and apprehensive. "You ain't gonna take my tobacco, are you?"

"In the bag," Fahrenthold ordered.

Anger stirred within Bass. He'd pinned on the U. S. Marshal's badge and taken an oath to stand against lawlessness in the Territories. Having to watch the other passengers get robbed was bad enough, but losing Nellie's gift would be more than he could bear.

He shifted his feet, setting himself to lunge.

"You don't want to do that," Alfred said quietly in Cherokee. "Maybe you'll get lucky and not get killed, but other folks will."

Bass let out a tense breath and met Fahrenthold's gaze as he slipped the jewelry case from inside his jacket.

"Why you're a big liar!" Fahrenthold exclaimed as he snatched the case. "Unless you carry your makin's around in a jew'ry box."

The robber opened the box to reveal the small silver bucking horse on a delicate filigree necklace. He snapped the case shut and dropped it in the bag.

"I'm sorry," his unwilling accomplice apologized. His eyes were wide and troubled.

"It's all right," Bass told the man. "You just stay safe."

With a shove, Fahrenthold got his helper moving again.

By the time the train started slowing down in the middle of nowhere, nearly all of the passengers had been robbed. Bass glanced out the window and saw nothing but rolling hills covered in red oak, scrub brush, and Indian Paintbrush flowers growing wild.

Another man wearing a neckerchief came into the passenger car from the forward cars. Like the others, he carried a long gun, an old Henry rifle that looked cared for.

"Time to go," the man growled. He turned and went back the way he came, but he stepped down from the stairwell toward the ground as the train ground to a halt.

As he stepped toward the door to follow the third robber, Eddie gestured with his rifle. "I was an army sharpshooter. Any one of you wanna see proof of that, just try stickin' your head out one of them windows while we're leavin'."

Passengers sitting near the windows drew back and ducked down so there'd be no mistake.

"I count nine of them." Alfred peered through the nearest window.

Bass gazed through the opening and counted the seven men who ran from the train to meet two riders waiting with saddled horses under a tall copse of hackberry trees mixed in with stands of elms and redcedars.

"I told you they had someone up with the train engineers," Alfred said.

"I didn't say they didn't," Bass replied.

"The other men were probably taking any payroll they came to get and robbing the other passenger cars."

"Think you can tear yourself away from the excitement long enough to act like a posseman now?" Staying low and carrying his hat in one hand, Bass walked between the seats toward the rear of the car and the baggage car beyond.

"Hey, they took my money too. I'm not planning to let them get off scot free neither." Alfred followed Bass out into the aisle despite some of the passengers telling them to stay down and cursing them for being up.

Outside, the train robbers clambered into saddles and headed their mounts north into the high and uncut.

"Was the train carrying a payroll?" Bass asked the young conductor he found in the baggage car a few minutes later.

In his early twenties and carefully groomed, the conductor stood in a daze in the midst of the debris that covered the baggage car. His uniform was neat and pressed, garters holding up his sleeves, immaculate except for the blood dripping from his burst lips and the split on his cheekbone.

"That's train business, sir."

Alfred stepped around the young man, lithely dodging the conductor's grasp at first, then grabbing one of the man's hands and turning it painfully inward to dissuade him from further attempts.

"I'm just getting my belongings," the posseman said. He rooted through the baggage and found his suitcase. He took out his Winchester rifle and a bandolier of rounds. Next, he pulled out a pair of dungarees, a faded brown flannel shirt, and a pair of well-worn boots. He stripped out of his suit and folded it neatly before replacing the clothing in the suitcase. Then he dressed once more in his trail garb.

Bass lifted his jacket to reveal the cartwheel shape of his Marshal's star. "I work for Judge Parker and I aim to find them men that robbed this train. Now tell me what they were after."

"It was a cashbox for Mantooth Benning."

"Who's he?"

"A banker up in Vinita."

Bass didn't know the man, but he'd had business in Vinita before. The town was first established and named Downingville, but it had been renamed Vinita in honor of a sculptor. Vinita attracted a lot of travelers because both the Katy line and the Atlantic & Pacific had railways there.

"That cashbox come through on regular times?" Bass asked.

"No sir."

"But these men came here looking for that cashbox?"

"First thing they asked about."

"They? How many men?"

"Two."

Bass glanced out the rear door window. Most of the passengers remained within the train cars, but a few men were stirring around now as the fear left them. The robbers had only been gone a few minutes. So far no shots had been fired.

"Do you know how much money was in the cashbox?" Bass asked.

The conductor hesitated, then he shook his head. "A lot I reckon."

"There wasn't any guards assigned to it?"

Blinking, the man nodded. "Three men. The robbers forced them to jump off the train." He licked his split lip. "I was going to jump too, but they made me open the safe." He swallowed hard. "I thought they were going to kill me."

"Well, they didn't, so you got through that fine." Bass found his own luggage, opened it, and pulled out his Winchester and his two Colt Model P .44 pistols. After changing into trail clothes and folding his suit, he strapped the gunbelts around his waist, one on each hip, butt forward, and added his spyglass to his kit. He kept the Winchester in one fist. "I'm gonna need you to see that these bags get settled at the Katy Hotel in Muskogee. Tell Mr. Briar, the manager, I'll be along for them quick as I can."

"Yes sir."

Bass headed for the back of the car. The train robbers had disappeared into the woods.

A tight knot filled his gut. He understood robbery. Men, and sometimes women, wanted something that didn't belong to them.

Taking Nellie's gift, though, made this hunt personal.

Bass knelt on the ground and used his forefinger to brush out the marks he'd found where the outlaws had joined up with their cohorts holding the horses. Trailing the men was easy at the moment. The ground was still soft from the light rain the previous night. Chunks of earth turned up by horseshoes stood out clearly.

At Alfred's approach, he rose and brushed off the knees of his worn dungarees.

"Engineer's got a lump on his head almost the size of my fist," Alfred said. He had several canteens strapped over his shoulder. "He's slow getting around, but he's getting there. He and the fireman think they can have the train moving again in a couple hours, so the passengers won't be stranded out here long. The man who busted the engineer up threw water into the firebox. It'll take time to clean it all out and get the pressure raised again in the engine."

Bass resettled his hat on his head, then reached down and grabbed the straps of four of the eight canteens Alfred had brought. Without another word, he turned and set off in the direction the outlaws had taken.

The faint crack of a rifle shot drove Bass to ground behind a large tree. He gripped the Winchester in both hands and peered north because that was the way the robbers had continued traveling.

"It's stupid hiding," Alfred called from a few feet away. He was lodged behind another tree. "If that bullet was meant for us, we'd have been hit before we heard the shot."

Before Bass could reply, another flurry of shots pealed around them. Three more shots followed sporadically behind those, then the forest was silent. Around them, the shadows grew long as the sun dropped in the west.

"How far away do you think those gunshots were?" Bass eased up from his position and studied the hilly skyline that lay before them.

"A mile, maybe, but not much more."

"That's what I'm thinking, too. Let's fan out on either side of the trail about twenty paces, keep it between us instead of following it directly. In case anyone's watching. If either of us crosses the trail, give a yell so we can stay with it."

Alfred nodded and stepped off to the left, almost vanishing in a swirl of greenery that closed behind.

Tense and fatigued, but every nerve alive, Bass followed his quarry. His mind constantly turned, wondering what had happened to the outlaws. A snake or taking game could account for two or three shots being fired, but a dozen or more implied some kind of battle had taken place.

Less than a mile ahead, the land rose again. The eastern part of the Territories was more like Arkansas's majestic tree-filled beauty in the Ozarks than the western part of the Indian Nation where the lands ran flat and open. Streams and rivers cut through the land here, and wildlife was plentiful.

Staying low, ascending in tandem with Alfred thirty feet to his left, both of them with their rifles in hand, Bass removed his hat and slowly extended his head up behind a squat evergreen bush. The needle-shaped leaves dragged along his whiskery jawline but didn't catch. He fetched his rifle up beside him and watched as three black crows sailed down from the blue sky with wings spread wide. They cawed loudly.

A horse stood near the forest's edge below. Its reins hung slack and dragged on the ground as it lazily munched grass. Less than ten feet away, a bloody body laid face up and unmoving on the ground as the crows pecked at the man's face. Twenty feet from the corpse, two more men lay sprawled on the ground and crows covered those as well. The white shirt on one of them revealed three bloody blossoms that Bass recognized as gunshot wounds.

Gingerly, he walked down the hill and stayed within the trees as much as he could while taking advantage of the cover they offered. The wind was in the horse's favor and the animal looked up when it caught Bass's scent. It whickered softly, twitched its ears, and flicked its tail. Its legs shifted and Bass knew the animal was ready to run. A worn saddle and blanket covered the horse's back.

Canting his rifle against his hip, Bass reached in his jacket pocket and held out a cupped hand to the horse. He carried a few sugar cubes in his jacket that he used to settle his own horses. The small squares stood out against his stained leather gloves.

"C'mon you."

After a moment, the horse plodded across the open area to the marshal. Bass took the reins as the horse ate the cubes and then nuzzled at his pockets for more treats.

Gently, Bass moved the horse with him, staying at the animal's side so that it shielded him from anyone hiding to the north where the bodies littered the ground. Cawing angrily, the crows pecking at the dead men took flight in a flurry of beating wings.

One of corpses belonged to the man who had entered the passenger car to tell Eddie and Fahrenthold it was time to go. Moving on to the next man, Bass flipped him over and studied his face, thinking he recognized the man from a dodger he'd seen. He stepped toward the third man.

A pistol cocked from somewhere on the other side of the horse.

Pulling quickly on the reins, Bass wheeled the animal around between himself and where the metallic clicks had issued. He slid the rifle up under the horse's jaw and tucked in close to the animal's thick shoulder.

"Put down that rifle an' I won't kill you," a hollow voice rasped from the shadows gathered under the trees.

Squinting a little in the dimming light, Bass made out the figure of a man tucked under the low limbs of a birch tree.

"I'm not putting my rifle down," Bass said, "and if you don't throw that pistol out, I'm going to shoot you."

"Who are you?"

"I'm United States Deputy Marshal Bass Reeves," Bass said.

"How'd you find me so fast?"

"I was on the train."

The man laughed. "Man, don't that beat all. Jelly had to go an' rob a train with a marshal on it, an' I had to be dumb enough to trust him."

"Where's Myron Eddie and the others?"

"They all lit a shuck for Vinita." The man coughed in a wheezing manner. "They kilt my pards an' tried to kill me."

"You're wounded?"

"Shot plumb to hell." A dry laugh followed, but it wobbled on the edge of hysteria.

"Maybe I can help you."

"Drop that rifle an' get over here."

"I'm not gonna do that."

"I'll shoot you."

"I like my chances here just fine," Bass said. "Don't look like you ain't gonna last long without somebody tending to you."

The man cursed and threw his pistol, but the weapon barely made it to the open area.

"Anybody else in the weeds?" Bass asked.

"Nope. Jelly left us all for dead." The man gave another wet cough that sounded weak. He cursed Myron Eddie till he ran out of air.

Cautiously, still holding onto the horse in case he had to mount and ride, Bass walked over to the man.

Lloyd Fahrenthold sat with his back to a tree and struggled to breathe. Blood covered his shirt from a couple bullet holes. More blood oozed down his face from a hole in his forehead. Bruising spread out from his forehead, along his nose, and turned his eyes into things that looked more at home on a raccoon.

"I remember you," Fahrenthold said, showing Bass a sour grin filled with bloody teeth.

"You're hurt pretty bad, Fahrenthold."

"You know me?" Fahrenthold looked surprised.

"I do." Satisfied no one else was in the area, Bass knelt down across from the man. "Care to tell me what happened?"

"Patch me up first."

"You've been gut shot. I could patch you up, but it ain't gonna do no good. You're a dead man." Bass had seen men die before and he could accept it, but watching it happen never got easy. Lying to a dying man was even harder, so he told the wounded man how it was.

Fahrenthold grimaced and cursed. "I ain't gonna die. You're wrong about that. You gotta get me to a doc."

"We're miles from anywhere," Bass stated. "I put you up on a horse, the ride will kill you and you'll be miserable the whole way. The best I can do is make you comfortable till you've passed on."

"Thought Jelly had kilt me for sure when he shot me in the head." Fahrenthold touched his head wound and his fingers came away damp with blood. "Bullet hit me, slid up under the skin, an' come out on the back side."

"Why'd Jelly shoot you?"

"Because he's greedy, may his soul burn forever on the devil's pitchfork!" Fahrenthold shifted and tried to sit up straighter. "Him an' his bunch went in pards with me an' my pards down in Muskogee. Wanted to take down the train an' needed more men."

"He came for the cashbox?"

"Yeah. *He* did." Fahrenthold cursed. "I didn't. None of my boys did. We only found out about it after we took everything off the train. When we got out away from the train, I called him on it. Me an' the boys wanted to know what we'd got our hands on. How much we were gonna get. Turns out Jelly was waitin' for us to get curious. They opened fire an' we went down." Leaning his head to the side, he spat blood. "I put a bullet in one of his boys. Hope I killed him. He was bleedin' enough, but they kept him set on that horse." He paused and swallowed. "Say, can I get a drink of water? I'm parched."

"Sure." Bass waved to Alfred.

"I wish one of those horses had been carrying a shovel." Bass laid another large rock on the newest fresh grave.

Fahrenthold had passed in the night, wheezing for air and crying out in pain. Bass hadn't been able to sleep and he hadn't been able to walk away. Watching the robber die in such an agonizing fashion hadn't been the worst thing he'd experienced, but it was the worst in a while.

Now, sleep-deprived and starving because he and Alfred had only managed to take a couple rabbits before sundown had arrived, Bass stood and rubbed his aching back. He wasn't a young man anymore, and all the miles in the saddle were taking their toll.

"I wish you'd have been happy just leaving those dead men where they fell." Alfred sipped from a canteen and stoppered it. He stood in the shadow of a tall oak on a small rise and kept watch.

"If we hadn't buried them, we wouldn't be able to dig them up again later to turn in for reward money. Fahrenthold and at least one of those other men has dodgers out on them."

"I'm thinking maybe carrying them back is going to stink so bad that

"I wish one of those horses had been carrying a shovel."

I'd be willing to take a pass on the money."

"I can come back by myself."

Alfred shook his head and sighed. "No. You'd just get lost without me to find this spot."

Stepping back, Bass surveyed the three fresh graves they'd cut into the ground. All of them were shallow, heaped over with dirt crawling with worms, and covered with rocks.

"I also wish you'd thought to bring some coffee from the dining car before we left the train," Alfred went on.

"And a pot to boil it in?"

"You can't drink coffee grounds."

Bass shook his head. "I got to say, I can't remember the time you was so fussy about things."

"I've told you before, back when we first met, how I feel about riding without a chuck wagon."

"Yeah, now that you mention it, I guess you've been fussy for a while."

Bass took his hat from a nearby tree branch and clapped it onto his head. He caught his rifle when Alfred tossed it over to him and walked toward the horses.

Last night, he'd managed to round up two other horses. They stood tied to a picket line under a spreading pecan tree and ate grass. Behind them, the sun poked a hole in a mass of bruised clouds and peered through the trees at the eastern horizon.

"Don't go fretting about the time we lost last night." Alfred picked up one of the saddles and carried it to a horse. "They picked this spot for a reason. They could have waited till we were farther down the rail line, farther west. Nope, they chose to stay around here."

"There's not much out here, and they weren't planning on going too far." Bass saddled his mount. "None of these horses had much in the way of supplies, and none of those men looked like they planned on living off the land."

"They'd have been disappointed if they had. All you can find around here is skinny rabbits. A man can exhaust himself killing and skinning them for a mouthful of stringy meat. And those robbers got that cashbox. They're planning on spending it somewhere."

"So where do you figure they're heading?"

Alfred tied his hair back with a leather string, then pulled on his hat. "My guess is Vinita."

"Why?" Bass pulled himself into the saddle.

"Can you think of anyplace else to go in that direction?" Alfred pointed to the north where the hoofprints led.

"No, but that still doesn't say why they're heading in that direction."

"Could be on their way to Kansas. Maybe they're planning on whooping it up there till they run out of money."

"Best I recall, Myron Eddie has worked around California, Colorado, and Texas. Seems more likely he'd head south."

"Maybe he's branching out."

Bass cursed at that and knew he wasn't going to get anything out of Alfred because neither of them knew what would be in the man's mind. He gave silent thanks that the rain that had threatened during the night hadn't come and washed away the hoofprints the outlaws had left.

Sitting atop his horse under a thick copse of trees on a low hill that overlooked the town below, Bass studied the streets and buildings through his spyglass. They'd spent the day following the train robbers and, after a handful of times spent doubling back to pick up the trail, he and Alfred had ended up here.

The town spread wide across the area. Main Street and the other avenues of the downtown area held churned ruts from recent rains. Vinita was growing, but the streets remained earthen.

Stone and wooden buildings lined the center of the town's thoroughfares. Wooden boardwalks fronted the businesses, which included a general store, a leather goods shop that showcased boots and saddles, and a café called Henry's Diner. Other shops housed a barber, a blacksmith and stable, an undertaker, a hardware store, a confectionary, and a dress shop.

Further inspection revealed more businesses, as well as four small banking interests—including Benning's, the tribal police office and jail, three hotels, and the Katy train ticket station. The population in Vinita was mostly Cherokee families.

Bass had been to the town on business before, the last time only a few months ago, but Vinita had already added on residences and shops. It was definitely growing quickly.

"Are we going to check in with the tribal police?" Alfred adjusted his hat.

"Nope." Bass pulled his gloves tighter. "We're gonna keep our heads low.

If Jelly Eddie and his boys feel safe hanging their hats here, there's a reason for that. I want to know what game's playing before we show our cards."

"Some of the tribal police will know you if they see you."

Over the years of riding for Judge Parker, Bass had crossed paths with the various lighthorsemen established by the Five Civilized Tribes. Bass respected the men that carried those badges. That said, as in most cases, not all of them were good men.

"Well," Bass said, "I ain't gonna be me."

"Name's Oscar." Bass stood at the back door of the Green Gate Hotel. Light from inside the establishment pooled over him and lit part of the alley around him. Trash barrels occupied space farther down and stank of spoiled meat and fermented fruit. "Oscar Drury."

The alias was one of several Bass had trained himself to step into when the need arose. Oscar Drury was an itinerant individual who knew horses and hard labor. He tended to be meek, didn't speak much, and had a tendency not to make eye contact. Bass had modeled the character after a murderer who had fooled him for weeks by pretending to be simple-minded.

"What can I help you with, Mr. Drury?" The hotel clerk was in his fifties, a Cherokee man with short cut gray hair and a neatly clipped mustache.

"I'm new in town." Bass paused because that was what "Oscar" would do.

The clerk waited for a moment, then, when he realized Bass wasn't going to continue, he sighed. "It's late, Mr. Drury. I've got a lot of work ahead of me and morning comes awful early."

"I'm sorry to bother you, sir, but I'm looking for a job." Bass continued to look at his rundown boots. He'd stopped at one of the small churches outside of town and purchased hand-me-downs from the preacher there.

"We don't have any openings," the clerk said. "I'm sorry."

"You don't gotta pay me much, mister. I'll work cheap. I'm just lookin' for a way to keep myself together a few days, get me a poke, then I plan on headin' on."

"I'm truly sorry, Mr. Drury, but I don't have anything for you." The clerk's apology sounded sincere.

The answer didn't surprise Bass. He'd been told the same thing at the diner, the blacksmith, and the leather goods shop. A job didn't matter so much. He just needed a way to blend in for a few days at most, just until he knew what Jelly Eddie and his crew were up to, and figured a way to arrest them for the train robbery.

"Well, thank you, sir." Bass nodded and stepped back from the door and the light.

The clerk started to shut the door, then caught himself and stopped. "Did you see the blacksmith's shop on your way through town?"

"I did, sir."

"He should be able to give you a place to sleep. I know that will be better than sleeping outdoors tonight."

"Yes sir."

"Tell them Mr. Croom at the Green Gate Hotel would appreciate him taking you in for the night. The hotel sends a lot of business his way."

"Yes sir. Thank you kindly." Bass kept backing into the shadows.

"Mr. Croom sent you, huh?" The rawboned young man wore overalls and an undershirt that looked like it would never come clean again. He was thirteen or fourteen and man-sized, still gaunt because he hadn't yet gotten his full growth. His dark hair hung like a raven's wing across his forehead. He held a lantern in his left hand and an ax handle in his right.

"He did." Bass nodded and didn't make eye contact. Instead, he swept the barn with his quick gaze.

The barn was adjacent to the foundry, which smelled of ash and hickory. A large anvil stood in front of the furnace in the center of the building. Hammers and tongs hung neatly on pegs on the wall.

The connected stable held paddocks for a couple dozen horses. Most of them were filled with dozing animals.

The boy looked past Bass at the horse standing behind him. "I can put you and the horse up. Got feed for the horse, but I want some help with the livestock in the morning."

"I can do that."

"Good. Then let's get you bedded down in the back." The boy turned and headed deeper into the barn. "It ain't much, I'm sorry to say. Nights my pap has me tending to late arrivals, I sleep out here myself. I got a cot. Makes it more passable."

"I cain't ask for much." Bass stopped as the boy halted in front of an empty paddock and gestured at the pile of hay inside.

"You and your horse can sleep here. I mucked it out myself tonight, so it's pretty fresh. Keep an eye out for mice. Got a ginger tom in here somewhere supposed to be keeping up with them, but there's a lot and he ain't greedy."

The boy took a lantern from the wall, lit it, and handed it to Bass. Then he said good night and headed back to his cot.

Bass took the saddle from the horse and got the animal bedded down with a feedbag. He held the light up for a moment and studied the surrounding horses. One of them had the same brand as his mount, letting him know there was a chance Jelly Eddie and his crew had arrived in Vinita too.

The boy got up before sunrise the next morning. Bass had no clue what had woken him because he hadn't heard anything. When the boy had grabbed his shoulder and shook him, Bass had automatically reached for one of his Colts, but the weapons were in his saddlebags.

"Time to rise and shine," the boy stated as he drew back. Holding the lantern up, he smiled down at the cat sleeping on Bass's chest. "I guess you found Ginger Tom."

"Guess he found me." Gently, Bass nudged the cat off him and sat up. He reached for his boots and pulled them on while the cat arched its back and stretched.

"My name's Robert," the boy said.

"Oscar," Bass said automatically. He stood and pulled his hat on. "Thank you for the bed."

"Now you got to earn it," Robert said. He gave directions for taking care of the horses in the barn.

While Bass helped feed and water the livestock, he inspected the horses, paying particular attention to the horses he found that shared the same brand as the one on the horse he'd ridden in on. One of them had matted blood on one haunch but no wound, and he remembered Fahrenthold's claim that he'd put a bullet in one of Jelly Eddie's men.

"Somethin' wrong?" Robert paused outside the paddock. Light was creeping in from outside as morning slipped in over the town.

Bass knew he had to tell part of the truth. He ran his fingers over the stiff patch of dried blood. "Thought this here horse was hurt. This is blood, but it ain't her blood."

The boy stepped forward and ran his fingers over the rust-brown spot. "It's blood all right." He frowned in thought. "Like you said, it ain't hers." He stepped back. "Ain't no problem of ours. Just a curiosity."

Bass fitted the horse's head into the feedbag of oats he'd brought for it. The animal settled in and started chewing without a care in the world.

"If you help me curry out the horses this morning, I'll stand you to breakfast over to Culver's. They set a fine table and serve out big portions. I can introduce you to somebody you can ask about work."

"All right."

The décor at Culver's Hotel was top-notch. The lobby furniture and rugs were clean and in good condition despite heavy traffic. Fresh flowers stuck up from colorful vases. The man behind the check-in desk was in his forties and wore an expensive suit. His slicked-down hair and muttonchops gleamed, every hair in place.

"That's Mr. Hester," Robert said as he guided Bass to the restaurant section of the hotel to the left.

Bass could have trailed the scent of strong, fresh coffee to the dining area, and the clanking silverware was a dead giveaway as well, but he followed Robert.

"You don't want to ask Mr. Hester about a job," Robert said as they entered the restaurant. "He concerns himself with the hotel's image too much. You want to ask Mrs. Delgado. She runs the kitchen and pretty much everything else here. She's got a kind heart."

A young woman in a nice gray dress escorted them to a table in the back.

Robert picked up one of the menus the serving girl had left and started looking it over. "You see something you like, that's fine, but don't spend too much. Neither one of us is rich."

Bass looked around at the dozen other tables where businessmen and ranchers sat taking their breakfast. Bass couldn't read, something he never advertised and ignored the menu. "Biscuits. Gravy. Steak or sausage. Eggs.

Milk, if they got it cold. And some coffee." He glanced back at the boy. "That okay?"

Robert nodded, and when the serving girl returned, he ordered for both of them and handed her back the menus.

Across the room, Alfred sat at a table by himself and drank coffee while reading a newspaper. Even as alert as he was, Bass almost missed the old man. Alfred was as good at disappearing in plain sight as Bass was.

The girl wasn't gone long before she returned with coffee for both of them, and a glass of cold milk for Bass. The food followed not long after. As they ate, Robert made small talk, mostly gossip about people in town he'd seen, and Bass guessed that the boy liked talking because he didn't give up on it even when his conversation company remained mostly silent.

While Bass was using a biscuit to mop up an egg cooked over easy that he'd spooned grape jelly into, two beautiful women entered the restaurant from the hotel lobby. A large man ushered them to a table in the middle of the room like they were specially designed centerpieces.

One beautiful woman would have drawn a lot of interest, but the two together had the attention of the whole room.

The older woman looked like she was in her late thirties, but she had to be older because the young woman next to her treated her with the respect of a child for a parent. The younger woman was in her early twenties.

Where the older woman's hair was blonde that had turned to alabaster, her daughter's blonde locks still held a deep honey color. The older woman kept her hair pinned back. The younger woman let her hair tumble past her shoulders.

The mother wore a white blouse and black pants with good shoes. Her daughter's blouse held a hint of lavender color and showed off her trim figure. Her dark yellow skirt made her look sophisticated, but it hugged her slim hips.

A serving girl quickly appeared and stood ready to take their order.

The man ordered for all of them, though he glanced at the older woman first. His wide face held rough features that had seen their share of bar fights and altercations. He was dressed in black broadcloth and a white French shirt.

"That's Miss Laura Fallon," Robert said. He stared at the young woman with avid eyes. "She usually eats breakfast in here with her mother every morning. Sure is a looker, ain't she?"

"Yeah," Bass replied. "She is." He managed a shy grin. "You sweet on her?"

Robert blushed and quickly glanced at his plate. "No. She just looks right through me. She's from Fort Worth, and I hear she's been to England and France. The Fallon family is rich. They own cattle ranches in Texas and in Kansas. Word is they're lookin' to buy land around here for another spread."

"Got any takers?" Bass knew he was pushing the Oscar cover thin, but he couldn't help himself.

"Mr. Mantooth Benning is supposed to be going in with her." Robert sliced another bite off his pancakes and pushed it through the pool of maple syrup on his plate. "At least that's what Pa says. I heard there was some kind of delay concerning Mr. Benning's money yesterday." He shrugged. "But that may not be the truth. People talk a lot, even when they don't know nothing."

Bass nodded. "Is that Mr. Fallon with them?"

"Nope. Mr. Fallon is dead. Long time back. Mrs. Fallon's been running things herownself. That man is Denis Charlet. Supposed to be a French name. He's sparkin' Mrs. Fallon, and he's also goin' in on whatever she's doin' here."

Deciding against asking any more questions, Bass worked on finishing his breakfast, but his mind stayed busy, thinking that maybe a lot more was happening in Vinita than most folks thought.

After breakfast, Robert introduced Bass to Mrs. Delgado. She was a small, quiet woman with a sense of humor and watchful eyes. She hired Bass as a hand for the hotel's small stable, which happened to rent paddocks from Robert's father, so Bass ended up working in the same place he'd awakened that morning.

The work proved simple enough and provided him enough free time to watch over people coming and going to the hotel. He still held out hopes that Jelly Eddie and his gang were somewhere around, and since the establishment seemed to be the hotbed of new business in Vinita, he thought it was the best place to be.

While he was combing out a big bay stallion with a blaze across its broad face, Alfred led his horse into the stable after talking briefly with Robert.

"The boy up front says you can give my horse a rub," Alfred said.

"How's the beds in that hotel?" Bass asked. His back still ached from his own night spent in the straw and the other on the trail.

"Like sleeping on a cloud," Alfred said. "Made that whole night of sleeping out under the stars night before last just go away."

"Glad to hear it." Bass removed the saddle from Alfred's horse and ran the currycomb across the animal's back.

"I can't tell you enough how good those beds are," Alfred went on. "I got up this morning feeling like a new man."

"I can see how it would be hard to pay attention to things what with your life being so easy."

"I have noticed that a lot of the horses in this stable have the same brand."

"Do tell."

"Yep," Alfred said, "and I can't help but think how unusual that is." He leaned against the paddock and watched while Bass worked on his horse.

"Do you plan on getting any work done?"

"Me?" Alfred smiled lazily. "Do you know who that brand belongs to?"

"No."

"Seems like something a fella in the horse business around here would know."

Bass peered across the horse's back and narrowed his eyes at the older man.

"Turns out," Alfred went on, totally unaffected, "the brand belongs to George Sheldon."

A quick rummage through Bass's mental files turned up the name quickly. "I've heard of him. We've investigated crimes linked to him, but we haven't ever proved anything."

"You missed a spot." Alfred pointed to the horse's flank.

"I didn't miss that." Despite his certainty, Bass ran the comb over the area again. "Sheldon's supposedly been involved in cattle rustling and running guns and whiskey, but we never could bring charges."

"That's because folks around him died off pretty quick when the law came around."

Bass ran the currycomb over the horse's rump and took note again of the old, gray scar on the animal's hide that signified ownership. "Sheldon's involved in the train robbery?"

"Either that or his horses have struck out on their own."

"You sure you got all this time for comedy?"

"I'm rested up," Alfred said. "Did I mention I had a good night's sleep?"

"Seems like you did. You saw the two women in the diner this morning?"

"Mrs. and Miss Fallon?"

"Yeah. Word is they're here to set up another ranch, but these are Indian lands."

"*Were* Indian lands." Alfred's words carried a note of disappointment and anger. "Some of them are being opened up for white settlers. And you can get around that if you pair up with Indian investors."

Bass thought about that as he ran the comb through the horse's mane. "Benning Mantooth is Cherokee."

"He is."

"And he's one of the people Mrs. Fallon and her daughter are pairing up with for their latest business opportunity."

"I didn't know that."

"I got a good night's sleep in the stable here and I learned that," Bass said. "Maybe those beds in the Culver Hotel aren't as beneficial as you think they are."

"I remain convinced."

"These horses belong to men who got in late last night."

"I'm thinking about working in a nap this afternoon," Alfred said, "but I'll be sure to keep my eyes peeled."

"You do that." Bass saddled the horse again.

At noon, Mrs. Delgado sent over a basket of fried chicken, biscuits, and greens for Robert, his father Simon, and Bass. From the way the blacksmith and his son acted, lunch like this wasn't a surprise. Since there wasn't a Mrs. Blacksmith and there appeared to be no Mr. Delgado, Bass suspicioned that the respective Mr. and Mrs. were keeping time together. There was also a strawberry pie, which cinched the deal.

The father, Simon, was a powerful man, made broad and heavy from swinging his hammer and working the bellows. He was quiet but had a good sense of humor, and Bass enjoyed their company as they told him stories, some of which might have been true, but Bass couldn't tell and it didn't matter.

Shortly after two in the afternoon, Miss Laura Fallon showed up at the stable dressed in riding breeches and a thick cotton shirt. Her handmade boots looked fresh from the leather goods shop. She wore her honey blonde hair pulled back under a cowboy hat. Cameo earrings caught the sunlight.

A trim, fit man at least ten years older than she trailed close behind.

His trail clothes looked new. His dark hair hung in a wavy mess. A Stetson hung on his back and he grimaced like he'd eaten something that hadn't agreed with him. He looked somewhat familiar to Bass, but he couldn't quite place the man.

Lauren Fallon marched past Robert to Bass. Her green-gold eyes flashed. "You're Mr. Drury?" Her breath was sweetly alcoholic.

Bass swept his hat from his head and held it in front of him. "Yes, ma'am."

"Well, Mr. Drury," Laura said, "I was told by the hotel concierge that you worked for the hotel guests."

"Well, ma'am, I reckon that's so."

"I want a horse saddled."

"Yes, ma'am. Which one you want?"

Laura strode past him. "The Morgan stallion back here, if you please."

Bass paused a moment, thinking that such a wild-spirited animal as the Morgan and a tipsy woman weren't a good match. "Is that your horse, ma'am?"

"I have permission to ride it from Mr. George Sheldon, who owns that horse."

The stallion was fifteen hands tall, a dun color, and had an evil temper. Bass had already experienced its wrath that morning while grooming it.

"Maybe you'd like to ride another horse, ma'am. That one's got the devil himself in it."

"No, Mr. Drury, I'll ride that one." Lauren crossed her arms. "Mr. Millard here doubts my ability to ride. I won't have that."

"Yes, ma'am." Bass grabbed a blanket, a bridle, and a saddle from the tack on the wall and headed back for the horse.

A few minutes later, Bass led the saddled stallion out of the stable and onto the street. Robert and Simon had paused in their work to watch from behind a fence wall and talked quietly together.

Taking leather gloves from her pocket, Lauren pulled them on while she studied the horse. She held a quirt she'd taken from the stable in the fold of her elbow.

"Lauren," Millard said. "You're going to get yourself hurt."

"I won't get hurt." Lauren nodded at Bass. "Hold the animal still, Mr. Drury."

"I want a horse saddled."

"Yes, ma'am." Bass set himself; the bridle clasped firmly in one hand, and held the horse in place.

The Morgan trembled slightly, its muscles quivering like a bowstring waiting to be loosed.

"He's gonna be purely rambunctious, ma'am," Bass warned.

"Hold that stirrup," Lauren commanded as she approached the horse.

Millard stepped forward and dropped a heavy hand on the young woman's shoulder. "Now you hold on, you little spitfire. I'm not gonna watch you get your neck broke an' have your mama mad at me."

Lifting her arm, Lauren swung the quirt at the man. The leather lashes whipped toward Morgan's face, but he caught his attacker's wrist and halted the blow.

"You ain't got any more chance of hittin' me than you do of stayin' on top of that horse, but I do like your spirit." Millard laughed at her.

Lauren struggled, but Millard's greater strength prevailed. When she tried to kick him, he pulled her into a too-familiar embrace, wrapping his big arms around her. She cursed in a most unladylike fashion.

"Mr. Millard," Bass said, "I'm gonna have to ask you to let Miss Fallon be."

Millard stared at Bass over the young woman's shoulder. "Back on outta here if you know what's good for you."

Back at the stable, Simon and Robert were hurrying around the paddocks.

Noting the pistol holstered at Millard's hip and the bleary look in his jaundiced eyes, Bass knew the entire debacle could go sideways quick. He didn't want anyone to get hurt.

"Mister Millard," Bass said with more steel in his voice, "let Miss Fallon go."

Millard cursed and reached for his pistol. The young woman raked her nails along Millard's whiskery neck, barely missing his eyes, spitting and snarling like a hellcat.

Just as Millard's hand closed around his pistol, Bass hit him with a large right hand and sent him stumbling backward. Dropping the Morgan's reins, Bass stepped into the man before he could recover his balance and used his greater size to shove him back again to keep him off balance. Bass clamped a hand over the holstered weapon and ripped it away.

"You just go on and cool off," Bass said as he shoved the pistol into his coat pocket. "I'll see that you get this back when you're sober."

Millard cursed a blue streak. Then his eyes widened as he looked over Bass's shoulder.

Wheeling at the sound of hoofbeats, Bass managed to step aside an instant before Lauren Fallon rode the Morgan through the space where he'd been standing. The stirrup caught him a glancing blow at his hip and drove him back as she and the horse passed.

Caught flat-footed, Millard raised his arms in self-defense, but the Morgan bowled him over, knocking him to the ground. He tried to regain his footing, but Lauren wheeled her horse around and came at him again. He dodged the horse, only just, but the young woman swung the brutal quirt and cut him across the face. Blood wept down his nose and cheeks as the horse turned on a dime. Flashing hooves cut divots from the hard-packed street in front of the blacksmith's shop.

"*Hyahhh!*" Lauren screamed as she drove the horse at Millard again.

Bass grabbed Millard's elbow and yanked the dazed man from the horse's path. He watched in disbelief as the young woman brought her mount around again in a tight turn, showing off excellent riding skills.

Shifting quickly, Bass pulled Millard into an awkward, lumbering run, though he knew he'd never get his charge to safety. At the last second, he yanked Millard from the horse's path. Lauren swung the quirt in passing and the leather strands whipped against Bass's cheek.

Eye blurring with tears, Bass held onto Millard and kept them both safe as the horse shot by. Knowing he had no choice when Lauren turned her mount once more, Bass pulled the captured pistol from his coat pocket and fired it into the air while the young woman readied herself to charge again.

"Ma'am." Bass leveled the pistol. "I'm gonna be obliged to kill that horse if you bring it this way again. Could be you'll get mighty banged up when it comes out from under you."

The young woman cursed and prepared to put her heels to her mount.

Then a strident voice rang out. "Lauren, stop!"

Across the street, Amanda Fallon stood imperiously on the boardwalk in front of Sahlberg's General Store.

At Bass's side, Millard wiped blood from his face and stood trembling. "Shoot her," he urged. "She's plumb crazy. Never seen the like. If you don't shoot her, she'll kill us both." He reached for the pistol, trying to claw it from Bass's hand.

Unable to continue any kind of fight on two fronts, Bass yanked his arm back, then cracked the pistol across Millard's skull, dropping the man unconscious in his tracks. If Lauren ran the stallion at them again, Bass didn't know if he could get Millard out of the way in time.

From the way she shifted in the saddle, Bass knew the young rider was planning to attack again.

"Lauren!" Amanda barked.

For a moment, everything hung, like a pistol hammer falling on a powder cap with detonation to follow.

Then, with another curse, Lauren wheeled the stallion around and rode between the buggies and wagons sprinkling the street.

"Mr. Drury," Amanda said, "when you have a moment, I'd like to speak to you at the hotel."

"Yes, ma'am," Bass answered.

Millard stirred and came around with a groan. He sat up and put a hand to the knot on his forehead.

"Mr. Millard," Amanda called. "You're fired."

"You cain't fire me," Millard said. "I work for Mr. Charet."

"Mr. Charet and I have an understanding," Amanda said. "He'll agree to my decision or he'll find himself a new partner. I think he'll treasure his agreement with me more than your service."

Millard tried to heave himself to his feet, but Bass placed a big boot on the man's thigh and held him in place.

"Don't get up right now," Bass advised, "or I'll crack you across the noggin again."

Cursing, Millard gave up the fight and lay back on the ground.

"I apologize for my daughter," Amanda said a half-hour later. She sat at a table in a small office behind the hotel desk in the Culver Hotel. Mr. Hester had arranged for her to use it.

Across the table from her, Bass kept his mouth shut and just listened. A man sitting quiet didn't make as many mistakes as one who kept talking when he didn't know what was going on.

"She's always been headstrong." Amanda picked up a cut glass bottle with an impressive label and poured more brandy into the snifter sitting in front of her. She glanced inquiringly at Bass, who nodded, and she splashed more amber liquid into his glass as well.

Bass sipped at the brandy, not really enjoying the too-sweet flavor.

"Her father and I had nothing when we got married," Amanda said. "We started up our ranch and never knew from one day to the next if we were going to make it. Thankfully, we did, but it was all through hard work and sheer cussedness."

Bass nodded.

"When Lauren came along," the woman continued, "we never wanted her to have to live the way we did. She grew up in that big house with everything a little girl could dream of. She was the apple of her father's eye." She paused a moment. "Josh loved that little girl, doted on her. And I did too. It's no wonder she grew up high-strung and spoiled." She smiled sorrowfully.

"I hear raisin' children is hard work." Bass said.

Straightening in her chair, Amanda regarded him. "Mr. Millard handled the horses and wagon for us, and he's no longer working for us."

"He works for Mr. Charet, he says."

"Perhaps he does and shall continue to do so, but he's certainly not going to be around my daughter and me any further. My daughter's taste in men is casual and flighty and oftentimes questionable. It's one of those things I have to put up with." Amanda frowned. "But I don't have to put up with Mr. Millard after today. However, I find that I am in need of a man who would be loyal and perhaps not so easily manipulated by my daughter. I would like to hire you, Mr. Drury, if you're so inclined. I no longer trust Mr. Charlet's judgment."

"I woulda thought you'd of had your own man for the job."

"I did. Unfortunately, Mr. Evans was robbed and killed in an alley only a few days after our arrival in Vinita."

"I'm sorry to hear that."

"Thank you." Amanda crossed her legs. "But let's talk about you, Mr. Drury. Are you interested in working for me? Maybe continuing to work for me when things here are finished?"

"I ain't ever been to Texas, ma'am."

Amanda smiled. "It's hotter there, but maybe the work won't be in Texas. I'm currently involved in talks here in Vinita for a new business venture I'm considering."

"Another cattle ranch? I've never been a drover, ma'am. Been a lot of other things, but never that."

"Actually, Mr. Charlet and some of the local businessmen and I are planning to open a rail line that we'll own. A spur to some lands around here and in Kansas so we can ship cattle on into Kansas City, Kansas. The days of driving large herds into Dodge City and Abilene are about over, what with all the farmers stringing up barbwire and this region turning to agriculture, I'm afraid. But we can run a rail line to tie into other railroads in the area. The Rocking F brand will continue to thrive."

Bass nodded. He was well aware of how the cattle industry was changing. It might not be going through its death throes, but they were definitely on the horizon.

"So what do you think, Mr. Drury?" Amanda asked. "Are you interested in the job?"

"Yes, ma'am. I am."

"Good. Then you're hired." The woman extended a hand and shook. Her grip was strong and sure.

"I heard you got a new job."

Bass looked up from the feedbags he was filling in the stable, getting ready for the evening feeding. The sun was already going down and twilight was overtaking Vinita's streets. Shopkeepers locked up for the night and went home.

Alfred led his horse into the building.

"I did," Bass admitted. "Turns out, it's the same work, just under different management."

"That's disappointing when it happens." Alfred tied his horse up, removed the saddle, and picked up currycombs from a nearby bucket. He worked on the animal with casual strokes.

"You've been out riding?" Bass asked, noting the dust that layered the horse's coat.

"I have. Did you know Mantooth Benning, Denis Charet, Amanda Fallon, and a few other successful business people here in Vinita have been buying up land?"

"I did." Bass put down the full feedbag and reached for another empty one. "Turns out they're planning a big cattle ranch near here, and building a rail line to handle it." He explained what Amanda Fallon had told him that afternoon.

"Something like that would take a lot of money."

Bass shoveled handfuls of feed into the new bag. "I hear they have it."

"Except maybe Mantooth Benning. On account of he got robbed. Good for him, though, because he's got more money. I heard he's got another shipment coming in tomorrow so he'll be able to get in on the deal. He's got a lot more guards this time, too."

"Maybe it'll make it here then."

"I think he's counting on it. Otherwise Charet's going to buy him out, and Benning doesn't want that to happen. Benning's been the one to do all the work setting up the land buyouts, using threat of the United States government opening up more areas to white settlers."

Bass glanced at his posseman. "Who have you been talking to?"

"Whitey Long. He's the head guard at Benning's bank."

"You just happened to meet him?"

"When I was in changing big bills for smaller bills. I figured next to the man who owns the bank, the man who guards it might know a thing or two about what's going on."

"And Long is just naturally talkative."

"Not so's you'd notice. Kind of tight-lipped, actually. You have to get him lubricated for the talking to happen. Fortunately, he's pretty open to getting lubricated once the bank's closed. Especially when he's playing cards at one of the private games here in town."

"You were playing cards?"

"When I wasn't napping and out riding the countryside."

"After such a big day, I don't see how you're still awake."

"It amazes me too, but I think it was all that rest I got last night. Did I tell you about the bed in the Culver Hotel?"

Bass sighed. "You might have mentioned it once or a dozen times."

"It was that good." Alfred smiled in obvious contentment. "Looking forward to it again tonight, to be honest. Maybe with your new job you'll get a bed too."

"I think I'll stay here with all these horses carrying the Sheldon brand. See if they go anywhere anytime soon. Jelly Eddie and his men came in on them. Could be they'll ride out on them again too."

"That's a good idea."

"I thought so." Bass reached for another bag. "Is Sheldon one of the investors?"

"No. Sheldon doesn't have the kind of liquid capital the investors are playing with, got his money wrapped up in real estate and small businesses, but he is pretty close to Charet."

"Is that so? With Charet being from out of town and new to the area?"

"I know. Surprised me too."

"How did they meet?"

"Over in France, the way Buchholz tells it, but Buchholz likes telling stories, so he might not know as much as he likes other people to think he knows."

"Buchholz?"

"He's a barber that a lot of the men who have money use." Alfred rubbed his chin. "Went and got me a store-bought shave today."

"I' m amazed at everything you've done."

"I know. No wonder I'm so tuckered."

Bass smiled, appreciating the old man. They worked well together.

"How do you want to handle this?" Alfred asked.

"I'm watching the Fallons."

"Heard the daughter is a handful."

Bass nodded. "She is. Man she was with today was assigned by Charet. I'm thinking we need to know more about him."

"I'll keep working my sources."

"Jelly Eddie and his men stole Mantooth Benning's payroll from the train, now they're here and came in riding George Sheldon's horses. I got to think that wasn't an accident. Wasn't any horse thievery announced, and the stable help ain't been told to look out for stolen horses."

"The horses do seem convenient."

"Look into both of Benning and Sheldon more, as quietly as you can, but I don't think Jelly Eddie and his people have come to Vinita to set up shop. Something else is going on, and likely it will happen sooner rather than later."

"I'll let you know what I find out." Alfred put the currycomb away and picked up his saddle.

"You know where to find me." Bass hoisted several of the feedbags over his shoulder and headed down the paddocks to tend to the horses.

For the next two days, Bass worked for the Fallons and kept his eyes open. That covered Friday and Saturday. During that time, he drove their covered carriage to fine homes inside town as well a larger, older houses in the country. Charet often came with them, but he rode a large black mare that Bass suspected had been chosen to complement his own look because the Frenchman wasn't a gifted horseman.

From the pieces of conversation he overheard, Bass knew the trips were made to talk to landholders Amanda Fallon and Denis Charet were negotiating with. Most of it was just pricing talk and trying to cajole key owners into selling or agreeing to long-term loans.

Lauren Fallon had taken up with a young banker, Clyde Fellowes, who worked at The Iverman Bank, the only financial institution larger than Mantooth Benning's bank. Bass kept tally of the people Amanda visited and knew that most of them banked with Benning.

Amanda wasn't successful in all of her dealings, but she did get most of the people to come around to her way of thinking. During the negotiations with her fellow investors, Amanda kept the upper hand. Bass listened to the discussions of the financial arrangements during the rides when Amanda talked with her daughter.

"Mother," Lauren asked Sunday afternoon, "are you certain you can trust Benning?"

"Why would you ask?" Amanda frowned at her daughter, and Bass caught the look from the corner of his eye.

"Because it's a lot of money."

"It's not your money. As I recall, you spent most of the money your father left you on frivolous things."

"I *traveled*, Mother," Lauren said sharply. "I learned things about the world you'll never know."

"I don't care to know those things. My life isn't going to be lived in those places. It's going to be lived in Texas, in that house your father and I built."

A strained silence followed for a time as the buggy creaked along back toward Vinita along the dusty road.

"Clyde says Mr. Benning isn't a trustworthy man," Lauren said. "That's why he quit working at Benning's bank and hired on to Iverson's."

"Clyde? You mean the young man you're seeing? Mister Fellowes? Why haven't you brought him around to dinner?"

"Clyde and I are courting. We have other things to do."

"Hopefully it will end better than your involvement with Mister Millard."

Bass cringed a little at that. There was nothing like a mother's ire toward her daughter, and he'd witnessed that firsthand at home.

"You're impossible," Lauren huffed. "You don't understand what it's like to be young and in love."

"Your father and I loved each other very much."

"You loved each other more than you loved me."

A sharp crack of flesh meeting flesh caused Bass to briefly glance over his shoulder in time to see Lauren shrink back from her mother.

"Don't you *dare* question your father's love for you," Amanda admonished. "Not ever."

"I don't question his," Lauren shot back. "I question yours." She looked at Bass. "Let me out here, Mr. Drury. I'll find my own way home."

Bass glanced at the young woman's mother.

"Please, stop, Mr. Drury," Amanda said. "If you don't, she will probably throw herself from the buggy. I don't want the horses spooked by her foolishness."

"Yes, ma'am." Bass pulled the team to a stop and started to get down to help Lauren to the ground, but the young woman simply vaulted over and walked away.

Bass seated himself once more, then, when Amanda nodded, he urged the team into motion once more.

"I'm sorry you had to see that, Mr. Drury," Amanda said softly. "She's every inch her father's daughter in some ways. Inflexible and determined, but she's so much more selfish than Josh would have ever thought about being."

"Yes, ma'am. Is she going to be all right?"

"She will be. She's carrying a pistol in her skirt. If I hadn't thought she'd be okay, I would have never let her travel abroad. And I would have trussed her up and brought her back to the hotel."

"Yes, ma'am."

Amanda leaned back in the buggy. "This is a pretty piece of country, but I have to admit, I'll be happy to get back to Fort Worth and my own home."

"From the sounds of things, don't seem like that will be long now," Bass said. "All the people you been talkin' to this last coupla days, you got most of your ducks in a row."

"I do. Even after Mister Benning's misfortune, we've got our money together. Thankfully, Mister Charet decided to join in our venture at about the same time."

"Mister Charet wasn't in on this with you from the outset?" That was interesting, especially considering his relationship with George Sheldon and his questionable New Orleans roots.

"Mister Charet is a cautious man."

"Seems like he's sweet on you," Bass said. "Pardon me if I stuck my foot in it. Sure don't mean to be tellin' you your business."

"I take no offense, Mister Drury." Amanda sighed. "Mister Charet *is* sweet on me, and I enjoy his attentions, but I'll never love another man. My husband was a unique breed. No, this is just business."

"Yes, ma'am." Bass thought of his own wife and the years they'd shared. He thought Nellie might have liked Amanda Fallon, but thinking of that

"This is a pretty piece of country, but I'll be happy to get back home."

made him remember the necklace Jelly Eddie and his gang had stolen, which took away some of the pleasantness.

While they were having dinner in his room at the Culver Hotel, Alfred reached into his saddlebags on the chest at the foot of the bed and took out a folded piece of paper.

"I've been meaning to show you this." Alfred smoothed out the paper on top of the small, square dining table the hotel staff brought up with the meal.

Bass spooned a bite of stew into his mouth and chewed thoughtfully while he studied the dodger. "That's Millard."

"No," Alfred said, trailing a finger along the writing that Bass couldn't read, "that's Herman Watson, a known associate of Gary Hickman."

"The man riding with Jelly Eddie that Fahrenthold said he wounded."

"Yes. After your run-in with him, I went and looked him up so I could remember his face. This morning, when I was looking through the dodgers at the tribal police department office, I happened on to this. Got more too."

Reaching back into the saddlebags, Alfred brought out seven more dodgers. One was of Myron "Jelly" Eddie and the others were of Hickman and five men named Wilson Orr, Kendall Avery, Chris Bohain, Keith Talley, and Sass Rubin.

According to Alfred, the men were known associates of Eddie.

"Eddie had five men with him when he robbed the train," Bass said as he turned over the possibilities. "That means three of these men might have been riding with him."

"That's what I was thinking," Alfred said.

"Watson might not have been one of the train robbers, if he was already here." Bass sopped a biscuit in his stew and tried to control his excitement.

"Working for Charet, you mean?"

"Yeah."

Alfred nodded and turned his attention to his meal. "Probably means all of them are here. And they're just waiting."

"Making us wait with them." Bass spooned up more stew. "I'm tired of waiting."

"You're just tired of sleeping in the stable. You're getting soft." Alfred smiled.

"Do you know where Watson is staying?"

"I do. There are some flop houses on the outside of town where the railroad track crews stay when they're in Vinita."

Bass took a drink of his milk. "Maybe we should ride out that way tonight. If you don't mind keeping that fine bed waiting a little longer."

The surprise raid Bass and Alfred conducted on the house where Watson was holed up might have saved a life or two. Watson and his cronies were deep into a whiskey bottle, certainly not their first of the evening, and deep into an argument about who was cheating whom at poker.

Five men, Watson and Hickman and one other face from the dodgers sat around a small table in the dining room. Coins and a few paper dollars littered the table. It wasn't much money, but Bass had seen people killed for less even when hootch wasn't involved.

"You boys put your hands up," Bass said in a deep voice as he stepped into the room holding his pistols. Like the train robbers had, he wore a kerchief up over his lower face as well as some different clothing. He didn't want to announce the presence of a United States Deputy Marshal at the moment.

Hickman, although wearing a sling holding his right arm, reached for his holstered pistol with his left.

Bass took a step toward the man and kicked him in the chest. Hickman hit the floor with a thump and his pistol sailed free only for Alfred to scoop it up.

"No more warnin's," Bass thundered. "Next man catches a bullet."

All of the remaining poker players put their hands up.

"You take that money," Watson threatened, his eyes just as jaundiced as they were the day he'd fought with Lauren Fallon, "we'll hunt you."

After holstering one of his pistols, Bass gripped Watson's shirt collar, hoisted Watson from the chair, and hustled him toward the door.

"They're going to talk," Alfred told the room. "You're going to wait here while they do. Everybody just keep your hands up."

Outside, Bass wheeled sharply on the short porch and slammed Watson into the wooden timbers of the rough wall. The wall shook and scraped Watson's face, leaving streamers of blood running down the outlaw's cheek and chin.

"What is Jelly Eddie doin' in Vinita?" Bass demanded.

"Go to hell," Watson snarled.

"I ain't gonna ask but this last time." Bass pushed his pistol barrel into Watson's ear.

Crying out for deliverance from the Almighty, Watson closed his eyes and cried out, "A bank job! Don't shoot me! He's here to do a bank job!"

"What bank job?"

"Benning's bank! A bunch of folks put all their money in his bank today! Part of some cattle deal! Him and Charles are gonna blow the safe!"

"Who's Charles?"

"Dennis Charles! Calls himself Charet! God, mister, don't kill me!"

"When are they gonna blow the safe?"

"I don't know. They're supposed to tell us." Watson trembled. "Stupidest thing I ever seen. Charles had Jelly and us rob the train so he'd have the money to rob the bank. We coulda just robbed 'em both, but he got greedy an' thought he could get in with that cattle woman too. So he took the money we robbed an' put it in Benning's bank. Now we gotta rob the bank just so we can get back the money we already robbed."

An explosion rocked the center of downtown Vinita. Stunned, Bass stared at the large gray cloud forming over the buildings. As he watched, flickering tongues of flame licked into being.

Watson jerked around and stared in disbelief. "What the hell? They started without us."

Bass reached into his back pocket for a piggin string and quickly looped Watson's hands together. He dashed inside the house to help Alfred with the others.

Minutes later, Bass drew his reins and brought his horse to a stop a short distance from Benning's bank.

The financial establishment was in ruins. Smoking chunks of the front wall and other debris lay in the street. People gathered around, talking and shouting, but no one ventured into the bank.

Benning ran up to the bank still dressed in his nightshirt. Bass recognized the man from the pictures Alfred had shown him in the *Indian Chieftain* newspaper.

Benning cupped his hands around his mouth. "Someone get water!

Hurry! I'll reward any man who helps save the bank!"

A few men broke ranks and hustled for water troughs and buckets.

Bass dismounted, pulled his kerchief from his neck, and plunged it into the water trough. As he wrapped it around his lower face to block some of the smoke from his nose and mouth, he plunged into the burning building.

He'd been in the bank before with Amanda Fallon, so he knew the general layout of the establishment. The smoke was so thick he couldn't see across the room in the flickering light. Flames crept along the ceiling and gained ground as Bass watched.

"Who are you?" a stern voice demanded. "What are you doing there?"

Bass turned and watched Benning step through the door with a lantern in one hand and a Colt in the other.

"Easy there, Mr. Benning," Bass cautioned. "I'm United States Deputy Marshal Bass Reeves. I work for Judge Parker out of Fort Smith." He held up his star and it glinted in the firelight. "I'm here after some bank robbers."

"Bank robbers?" Benning remained in the doorway. "You mean arsonists. Somebody set my bank on fire."

"Somebody blew up your vault, sir. Didn't you hear the explosion?"

"What are you talking about?"

Bass walked to the rear of the bank. Thankfully most of the fire was contained in the upper floor for the moment, though it was eating its way through.

At the vault, the heavy door hung partially open on twisted hinges. On the floor in front of it, a man lay torn in pieces. Blood had sprayed across the varnished hardwood.

"Who is that?" Benning demanded.

Alfred snatched the lantern from the banker in passing and crouched beside Bass. "That's Charet, or Charles, whatever you want to call him. You can tell by the stench of that cologne."

Bass silently agreed, but he took in the man's size too, matching it against his memory of Charet. Everything corresponded with what he remembered of the man, including the clothing.

"Looks like he caught the brunt of the blast," Bass said.

"The door or the explosion?" Alfred asked.

"Maybe both." Bass coughed and stood, looking around the room. "Did he come alone?"

"I don't see anybody else." Alfred swept the lantern around the room.

"Seems like Jelly Eddie would be here somewhere," Bass said. "Charet wouldn't have come to rob the bank by himself. He couldn't have carried it all away on his own."

"Somebody did!" Benning shouted. "All my money's gone!" He stood at the yawning mouth of the vault and held up a burning match.

The scant illumination revealed a small scattering of paper bills quietly burning like autumn leaves.

Stepping through the ranks of the volunteer fire department that had formed in the street in front of the burning bank, Bass swept the sea of faces with his gaze. Alfred walked beside him, both of them easing through the bucket brigade and the line of gawkers.

"You think Charet tried to cheat his gang and blew himself up doing it?" Alfred asked.

"If he had done that, the money would be there," Bass said.

"Not if Benning took it out of the vault in the first place."

"You've got a suspicious mind."

"It's the company I keep."

Bass grinned. "Then you come by it honest."

He circled the bank, weaving through people and watching faces, looking for Jelly Eddie, George Sheldon, and their possible cohorts. He concentrated on ways the bank's money had disappeared, thinking it was too coincidental for it to have vanished the day all of the funds were in place.

He didn't think Benning was in on the robbery. The man wasn't that good of an actor. Benning was genuinely distressed, still caterwauling about the loss over the noise of the fire and the rescue efforts. Watson and his poker buddies were tied up, literally, shortly after the explosion broke open the vault.

"I got something here," Alfred called out.

The posseman stood near the back of the bank. When Bass joined him, Alfred held up the lantern he'd taken from the banker and pointed to the smear on the brick.

"Blood," Alfred said. "Plenty of it." He put his hand up next to the smear to show that it was larger than his palm. He pointed down to the ground, indicating more splotches there. "Whoever it was, he was bleeding like a stuck hog."

Bass rounded the building to the alley behind it. Flames jumping through the bank's roof illuminated the narrow area like twilight.

Alfred toed ruts in the dirt floor of the alley. "These look fresh. And the hoofprints are definitely a late occurrence. The light rain this afternoon softened the ground but didn't go deep. Part of this is as dry as powder."

Something glinted in the lantern light, and it confirmed Bass's suspicions. He knelt and picked up a dainty earring with an ivory cameo, letting it hang between his fingers.

Then he closed his hand over it and stood. He noted the pool of blood on the buggy tracks, guessing that he wasn't the only one who knew what was going on.

Mr. Hester at the front desk started to object to Bass heading up the wide stairs to the hotel's upper floors. Bass showed the man his marshal's badge and backed him off, but the clerk didn't go without a sour look of disapproval.

Alfred walked at Bass's side. Both of them carried their rifles in hand.

Bass rapped on the door to room 303.

"Who is it?" Amanda Fallon asked.

"It's Mr. Drury," Bass answered. There was no need to confuse things from the outset.

The door opened to the length of the security chain.

Amanda looked up at him. "What can I do for you, Mr. Drury? I heard Benning's bank is on fire."

"It is for a fact, ma'am. It got robbed, blowed up, and caught fire."

"You're here to tell me that?"

"No, ma'am. I need to come in so we can talk about who robbed the bank and killed Charet." Bass held up his star.

"You're a deputy marshal?"

"Yes, ma'am, and I'm coming through that door whether you open it or not. It would be better if it was open."

"All right." Amanda closed the door slightly, although Bass kept his boot ready, and unfastened the chain. Once the chain fell away, the door swung open. "Come in, Mister...I suppose it's not Drury, is it?"

"No, ma'am." Bass stepped inside. "It's Reeves. Deputy Marshal Bass Reeves." He glanced around the finely appointed hotel suite. Amanda and her daughter had been living in the lap of luxury. "May I ask where your daughter is?"

"I'm afraid she's not here." Amanda looked slightly nervous, but her gaze was steely.

Bass nodded to Alfred, who quickly entered and started searching the rooms.

"Hey," Amanda said, going after the posseman, "you can't—"

"He *can*, Mrs. Fallon." Bass gently caught the woman's arm and halted her. "We're here on marshal business."

"Surely you don't think *I* had anything to do with the bank robbery!"

"Not you, ma'am." Bass released the woman and held up the cameo earring. "Your daughter. I found this out in back of the bank, and—unless I miss my guess—the buggy tracks I found there will match up with your buggy."

Color drained from Amanda's face as a look of betrayal filled her features. "The bank robbery, if there was a bank robbery, will be under the purview of the tribal police, as I understand the law here. Not you."

"Only a matter of time till the bank robbery got handed over to me. I'm just cutting out all that time wasted in the middle." Bass dropped the earring back into his pocket. "And it wasn't a bank robbery that brought me here. It was a train robbery. I'm tracking at least one of those men now, I believe."

A shrill scream of defiance came from the other room, followed immediately by a brief scuffle of blows and slaps. A moment later, Alfred pushed Lauren Fallon into the main room ahead of him. Her hands were bound behind her back.

"Lauren…" Amanda whispered. "What have you done?"

"Nothing," Lauren shouted. "What is going on?"

"Game's over," Bass said, and took out the earring to show her. "I found this out in back of the bank just now. I remembered them from when you rode Mr. Sheldon's horse a few days ago."

"That doesn't mean anything!"

"Where's Mr. Fellowes?" Bass put the earring back in his pocket.

"What does Mr. Fellowes have to do with this?" Amanda demanded.

"You were courting Mr. Fellowes," Bass said to Lauren. "He used to work for Mr. Benning at the bank. I'm betting you used him to get you into the bank tonight."

Lauren just smiled at him.

"Tell me what happened at the bank tonight," Bass said. "Maybe I can convince Judge Parker to show you some mercy at your trial."

"What trial?"

"Your murder trial. Mr. Charet was killed during the robbery."

Laughter glinted in Lauren's wild eyes. "Are you sure he didn't get killed while blowing up the bank vault?"

"I'm sure," Bass replied. "He was a careful man. His real name was Dennis Charles, and he was an outlaw wanted in New Orleans."

A look of shock passed over Amanda's face.

"Your mama didn't figure it out," Bass said, "but I'm betting you had a clue."

"I knew he wasn't what he said he was," Lauren replied smugly. "I've heard real French accents. His wasn't."

"She's got Charet's cologne all over her," Alfred said. "Could be she talked Charles into going there with her tonight. To look at all that money or something."

"Lauren!" her mother cried.

"Oh shut up, Mother!" Lauren exploded. "That's what shocks you? That I could steal the attentions of some man you thought was wrapped around your finger?" She fought against her bonds, but Alfred held her in place. "Please. That was so easy."

Scarlet clouded Amanda's face, but Bass thought there was more pain than anger there. The betrayal by a child was a terrible thing to endure.

"I'm glad your father never had to live to see you like this," Amanda said hoarsely.

"He wouldn't have cared." Lauren glared at her mother. "All you two ever cared about was each other. And your money. Both of you just kept it away when it could have been used to see the world. Like *I* did."

"Till you ran out of money," her mother replied. "You were always so short-sighted."

"I stole all of your money," Lauren crowed. She laughed. "You know, the funny thing is that I stole it just ahead of Charet. He took me there tonight to steal that money. That was his plan all along, don't you see? He was going to take everything and run."

"Lauren, don't say anything..."

"When he and his man Myron Eddie were putting nitroglycerin in the vault door," Lauren raised her voice to be heard over the protestations of her mother, "they didn't know that Fellowes was waiting in the bank for me. Fellowes shot Eddie while he was pouring his explosive into the drilled vault door." Her eyes turned wild again and she laughed. "It caused the most tremendous explosion, Mother! You should have seen it! The vault door careened into Charet and smashed him!"

"Where's the money?" Bass asked.

Lauren glared at him. "I'm not going to tell you."

Bass tried another tack. "Where's Fellowes?"

Lauren shrugged and shook her hair back.

Frustrated, Bass tried to think of what to do. There was no other pressure he could put on the young woman.

"Fellowes is dead," Jelly Eddie said as he stepped into the room from the adjoining room. His clothing was burned and ripped, and his eyes were bloodshot. Crimson stained the left side of his face and his shirt sleeve.

Bass turned and tried to raise his rifle, but Eddie stepped behind Alfred and pointed his weapon at Amanda.

"Put your gun down, Marshal, or I'll kill the old lady, then put a bullet through this Indian's head."

"All right." Bass gently bent and placed the Winchester on the floor, expecting a bullet at any moment. "What do you mean, Fellowes is dead? Did you kill him?"

Eddie laughed. "Not me. This little hellion here. I found him shot in the back of the head in the buggy they drove out of the bank. They'd already loaded up the money by the time I got there." He looked at Lauren. "Maybe you don't have to tell the marshal where the money is, but you'll tell me. I guarantee it."

A sharp *crack!* split the sudden silence that had descended over the room.

Bright blood bloomed where Eddie's right ear had once been. Crying out in pain, he pointed his weapon at Amanda, who was already easing back the hammer of the small derringer she held. Evidently Lauren wasn't the only one who carried armament in her skirts.

Bass pulled his rifle to his shoulder, sighted, and squeezed the trigger. The bullet smashed through Eddie's forehead and spilled his body back onto the floor.

Taking advantage of the confusion, Lauren kicked free of Alfred and tried to grab the fallen outlaw's Colt.

Amanda fired again, and her bullet smashed into Lauren's shoulder. Crying out in pain, the young woman looked at her mother in disbelief.

"You shot me, Mother!"

"Not to kill," Amanda stated as she reloaded the hideout gun. "Not this time, but if you try for that pistol again, so help me, I will. I'd rather bury you than watch you hang. And you will hang for what you've done."

Alfred eased over, picked up the Colt, and slipped it into his belt.

Slowly, Bass walked over to Amanda and gently plucked the derringer from her hand. "If you don't mind, Mrs. Fallon, I'll take this."

She didn't fight. Instead, she quietly walked to the nightstand, took out a bottle of bourbon that was contraband in the Territories, and drank it straight.

Bass didn't blame her.

The next morning, feeling worn to the bone, Bass sat outside the Vinita telegraph office and waited for a reply to the message he'd sent to Judge Parker's office. He watched foot traffic going by, most of them idling to stare at the burned remains of Benning's bank.

After a few minutes, Alfred crossed the street from the Culver Hotel carrying two cups of coffee. He handed one to Bass and sat on the bench in front of the telegraph office.

"You don't look so perky," Alfred commented. "After sleeping on one of those hotel beds last night, I figured you'd look better."

"Last night?" Bass shifted on the bench. "I didn't get to bed till six this morning."

"Well, then maybe you should have just stayed up." Alfred blew on his coffee and took a sip. He'd slept short hours too, but he looked refreshed.

They'd spent most of the night getting the right people locked down in the tribal police jail, and locating the stolen money, which hadn't been that hard to find when they had time to look for it. Lauren had hidden it in the stable. She'd left Fellowes and the buggy in an alley a few blocks away, then headed back to the hotel and her mother.

Bass wasn't sure what the young woman's plan had been to get away. She still wasn't talking.

Amanda Fallon wasn't saying much, and it was apparent the money didn't matter. She was already shutting down the deal she'd had in place, not even waiting to see if it would go through now. She only told Bass she wanted to return to Texas.

Still, not everything had turned out badly. Jelly Eddie had been carrying Nellie's necklace in his kit, along with some other pieces of jewelry Bass intended to return to the rightful owners.

"You know," Alfred said, "we're going to be taking a lot of people back to the judge."

"I know, and both of us will get big paydays. I think we'll be able to stay a while when we get there." Bass dangled the bucking horse figurine between his fingers and watched it sparkle. "I'm looking forward to that."

THE END

A TOWN CALLED VINITA

Maybe my heroes haven't always been cowboys, but man there have been a lot of them. Even the comic books I read had the original Ghost Rider, which they retconned to Phantom Rider, who had a cape and a mask!

I grew up on Louis L'Amour, Luke Short, and a ton of writers who wrote for Ace Western Double. I read those at about the same time I discovered the Ace Science Fiction Doubles, so I can't really say which came first.

I enjoyed my first Bass Reeves story a lot, so when the opportunity arose for a second one, I was thankful. I started looking around in Oklahoma history, finding things that appealed to me.

One of the strangest things we have in Oklahoma is the McDonalds in Vinita, Oklahoma. It stretches across both sides of Interstate 44. Go ahead and look it up on the internet. Think about walking the long way to get a Quarterpounder.

So I looked up Vinita, dug into the history. I found out that the city was one of the first in Oklahoma to get electricity and it was home to Tom Threepersons, a Cherokee lawman who is thought to be one of the last gunfighters of the Old West. He even invented a fast-draw holster that is still used with lawmen today.

As I read about Threepersons, I really wished I could find some way to incorporate him into the story. Unfortunately, he wasn't born until 1889, which would have fit into my tale of an older Bass Reeves, but I couldn't find a way to shoehorn Threepersons' future history into the tale.

But Tom Threepersons and his amazing life bumps around in the back of my writer's mind, so maybe one day I'll just do a story about him.

Until then, I had this tale, and I had a good time. I love the way Bass and Alfred Tubby come alive on the pages as I write down their adventures. They're two guys who've been through a lot together and have figured out how to get things done. And still share a joke now and again. They have some laughs in this one, even though things get pretty serious along the way.

I love writing Westerns because the land is beautiful, the stories are simple, and the stakes are always so high!

MEL ODOM - grew up in southeastern Oklahoma, where diehard country boys still eat possums and soft-shelled turtles, but now lives in Moore, Oklahoma, a wonderful town that unfortunately attracts Pecos Bill riding a twister on a regular basis. He's lived through hog raising and F-5 tornados, surely two of the most dangerous things in the world.

Over the last twenty-plus years, he's written dozens of novels in many different genres, including some based on television shows like *Buffy the Vampire Slayer* and novelizations of *Blade, Tomb Raider,* and *xXx.* He's trekked through deadly forests and braved the Sword Coast in the Forgotten Realms, and written adventures of bioroid detectives in Fantasy Flight's Android game.

He teaches in the Professional Writing program at the University of Oklahoma and writes all the time. He can be reached at mel@melodom.net, www.melodom.blogspot.com, @melodom on Twitter, and on Facebook.

His current military science fiction trilogy, *The Makaum War,* has been hitting bestseller lists.

THE PLEDGE

by Michael A. Black

1879: The Indian Territories

Four horses paced about nervously within the confines of the corral. Beyond the enclosure, perhaps thirty yards away, a trail of smoke wound out of the chimney. Bass Reeves moved up through the fencing of the corral, pausing to pet one of the nervous horses on the neck, while still keeping his eyes on the ramshackle house. He was a big man, over six feet, and powerfully built, but he moved with the grace of a big feral cat. Many of his Indian friends referred to him by the name Dark Panther, which Reeves found amusing, given the color of his skin. Two saddles had been haphazardly slung over the uppermost rails of the fencing nearest the house. That meant two riders. At least two, perhaps more. But given the proclivity of the two Gunther boys for taking what wasn't theirs, Reeves harbored little doubt that at least two of the four steeds were most likely stolen. A privy was on the left side, about twenty feet from the dilapidated house. An equally decrepit barn sat about a hundred feet to the right. The front doors were standing open and Reeves could see spots of the fading sunlight dappling the barn's floor through the numerous holes in the roof. The horse relaxed under Reeves's practiced grip. He knew horses as well as he knew men, and he urged the beast forward using its bulk to obscure his movements. As he got to the end of the fencing the front door of the cabin opened and a man strolled out, pausing to lean against the door jamb to pull on his second boot. The man was clad in filthy longjohns, but had his gunbelt strapped over his hips. Straightening up, he looked around. Reeves stood still next to the horse. It would be movement, either by him or the horse, that would betray his position.

The man in the underwear, whom Reeves assumed was Billy Gunther, the younger of the two wanted brothers, spat on the ground and headed for the outhouse. Reeves let his eyes peer to the side, following the man's movements.

Billy Gunther pulled open the door to the privy and stepped inside. Reeves moved cautiously to the edge of the corral and watched the house.

The door remained closed, no sign of movement inside. He glanced toward the outhouse again and saw his Indian deputy, David Walks-as-Bear, was a few yards away from it pointing his Winchester 1873 rifle at the wooden door. Reeves held his hand up, palm down, signaling Bear to wait.

No sense disturbing a man when he's taking care of that kind of personal business, Reeves thought with a smile. Besides, it was better that he be cleaned out as good as possible. The trip back to Fort Smith in the wagon was challenging enough without having to smell a pair of soiled longjohns the whole way.

Still, both Billy and his brother, Joseph, were hardened killers. Judge Parker's warrants read dead or alive, or so Reeves had been told. He was illiterate and had to commit the names and particulars to memory. It would be easier to take Billy by surprise, shoot him while he was in the privy, and not risk a confrontation. Both brothers had killed numerous men, and shown no compunction about shooting lawmen. But shooting a man without first giving him a chance to surrender wasn't what Reeves thought proper. He had been given the position as deputy marshal by Judge Parker, who had stressed that upholding the law was paramount. "Even the white man's law?" as one Reeves's fellow Negroes asked him. "The law ain't perfect," Reeves had answered back. "But it's all we got." He'd given his word, his pledge, that he would uphold it to the best of his ability.

That meant bringing them back alive to stand trial, if at all possible.

Reeves stooped and slipped through the wooden rails. The ground leading up to the house was dry and barren. Tuffs of stubborn field grass had managed to pop out in spots, but the area had been trampled by uncountable horse tracks.

Something moved inside the house. Reeves froze where he was, glancing left to check on Bear. The Indian's buckskin jacket and dark pants faded into the shadow of a solitary oak tree. No need to worry about him, but Reeves had no cover between him and the door, which suddenly opened.

A large man stepped through rolling a cigarette. It was the older Gunther brother. He wore his pistol slung low on his leg, the mark of a gunfighter.

Reeves withdrew his own Colt .45 Peacemaker and held it down by his leg.

Gunther must have caught the movement because he looked up and grinned, still holding the rolled cigarette.

"Joseph Gunther," Reeves said in a loud voice. "I'm Deputy Marshal Bass Reeves. I have a warrant for your arrest."

Gunther smirked and placed the cigarette between his lips. "The hangin' judge sent a nigger to get me?" He shook his head and snapped a match with thumbnail. He raised the match with his left hand toward the cigarette, while his right hand darted for his gun. He had barely cleared leather when Reeves brought his own revolver up, cocking back the hammer, and extending his arm. He squeezed the trigger and saw Joseph Gunther twist with the impact of the round. Gunther fired a shot, which Reeves felt zing by him. Reeves cocked back the hammer again, and fired. This time Gunther doubled over. Another round from his gun discharged harmlessly into the dirt. As he twisted and fell forward, the door of the outhouse burst open and Billy Gunter emerged, firing his gun wildly, the trapdoor of his longjohns still unbuttoned, hanging down in back.

Reeves turned and centered his weapon on the younger Gunther. The bullet caught Billy in the throat and his head jerked back. He seemed frozen for a split-second, and then lurched sideways as the roar from Bear's Winchester rifle sounded. Billy Gunther flopped down on the ground, face-first.

Reeves turned his attention to the prone Joseph and approached the downed man carefully. Playing possum was a technique that Reeves had seen before, and the lawman was always aware that a man was still a danger until you knew he wasn't. He trotted toward the older Gunther at an oblique angle, affording himself a bit of an advantage should the outlaw suddenly come to life. As Reeves grew closer, he could discern the man's ragged breathing. Gunther's hand still clutched his weapon, a long-barreled revolver, but he made no move to use it. Reeves covered the remaining distance and kicked the gun from Gunther's fingers. The outlaw's other hand was empty and Reeves flipped the man over. Twin holes, one high on Gunther's chest and the other lower, on his right side, leaked crimson. The blood from the lower wound was dark, telling Reeves that the bullet probably hit the man's liver. It was the end of the trail for this one. Reeves glanced toward Bear, who was standing over the younger Gunther brother, the barrel of the big Winchester rifle pointing down at the outlaw. Bear returned the look, shaking his head.

"My brother Billy dead?" Gunther said, his words laced with pain.

Reeves nodded.

Joseph Gunther closed his eyes and Reeves thought he saw a tear start to work its way down the outlaw's cheek. "Damn," the man said. "Never thought it would turn out like this."

Reeves watched as Bear moved past them and toward the house.

"Anybody else in there?" Reeves asked. "Nobody else has to die."

Gunther shook his head.

Bear leveled his rifle and kicked open the door, entering the cabin. He emerged about thirty seconds later and nodded.

"It's clear, Dark Panther."

Reeves turned his attention to Gunther, who was writhing in the dirt. "Never thought one of your kind would be able to best me," Gunther said.

Reeves shrugged. "It was your choice. I gave you a chance to surrender."

"I fought with the Confederacy durin' the War," Gunther said. "You?"

"I was in it," Reeves said.

Gunther nodded. "You're a brave man, I'll give you that."

"I promise to give you and your brother both proper burials," Reeves said. "If'n you have any valuables you want returned to you family, tell me now."

Gunther licked his lips, shook his head.

"We ain't got nothing," he said. "Reckon you'll take them horses. We stole 'em anyway." The outlaw stopped and coughed, sending a wet patch of blood dribbling down his chin. "I'd be grateful if'n you bury me and my brother side-by-side, Marshal." He coughed wetly again, then pointed to his pants pocket. "I got me my father's watch here. Promise me you ain't gonna steal it. It'd give me comfort going to my rest and knowing it was with me."

"I'm a lawman. I don't steal."

Gunther closed his eyes, took two quick breaths, then grimaced in pain. "You can… take my gun… It's a good'n." He motioned with his right hand. "Presented to me by none other than Jessie James. I kilt ten men with it. Want you to have it."

Reeves looked down at the weapon. It was the kind popular with many outlaws, a long-barreled .45 Remington 1875.

"I can't do that," Reeves said.

"Sure you can, Marshal," Gunther said. His lips twisted into something akin to a smile. "I want you to have it. Please. You're a good man… Better than me, even… I…"

Gunther stiffened, never finishing the sentence.

Reeves moved the tow of his boot against the outlaw's open eye. It didn't flinch.

"Looks like another dead one, Dark Panther," Bear said.

"Will you quit callin' me that?" Reeves said.

Bear smirked. "I thought I told you. Some of my people are from the north… Potowatomi. It is their custom to refer to great and noble warriors by their spirit names, and yours means…"

"I know what the hell it means," Reeves said. "You keep reminding me often enough. Go rustle us up a couple of shovels. We got us some burying to do."

"Okay, Dark… Boss.

Reeves jumped forward and kicked the Indian in the rump. Bear emitted something halfway between a yelp and a laugh as he shuffled off toward the barn.

Temptation, Population 147
The Indian Territories

Julian Henry Buckner, the Third, jumped down from the open buckboard and onto the dusty street. He reached into his pocket, found a nickel, and handed it to the driver. The old man flashed a gap-toothed grin, and smacked the reins on the haunches of the two horses. Buckner was barely able to grab his traveling bag before the buckboard jolted forward.

Idiotic lout, thought Buckner. He could have at least waited until I'd removed my luggage. And one would think that the railroad would have provided more accommodating transportation for such a long ride from their rail stop location. It had to be twenty-five minutes of wind and dust.

The wagon wheels stirred up more clouds of dust, and Buckner stepped back as best he could. Not that there was any sidewalk to speak of. He looked around. The town consisted of two blocks of buildings, most of which appeared to be in need of some upkeep. There were decrepit stores offering canned food and other sundries for sale. A few people, looking like families, eyed him warily from the confines of the stores and a few other buildings. They looked timid and meek. Buckner resisted the temptation to let out a ferocious snarl just to see if it would frighten them back into the shadows like scared mice. He walked by a telegraph office, but it was unoccupied. The only two-story building was the hotel, which looked in dire need of a coat of paint, and it sat across the street from the bank, which appeared to be the only brick and mortar building in the city of Temptation.

Buckner smiled. This place could hardly be called a city, even by a fiction writer like himself. But as he headed down the street he began framing the description for his next dime novel.

The town of Temptation was located in what had become known as the Indian Territories… Home of five tribes and countless outlaws.

He'd have to look up what those Indian tribes were, but overall, he liked the phrasing and longed for a chance to stop and commit it to writing before the muse deserted him.

The streets were deserted, even though it was early evening, he continued in his literary mind's eye. *However many decent people there are left, the wagon driver had told him on the way from the railroad stop, know better than to show themselves once the sun starts going down.*

Great stuff, he thought.

The sound of raucous laughter filtered out of one of buildings and Buckner headed right for it. A crudely painted sign above a pair of batwing doors read: *TEMPTATION CITY SALLOON. NO NIGERS OR INJUNS ALOWED.*

Buckner was mildly amused at the poor spelling, but not totally surprised at the sentiment expressed. He'd heard that this was basically a lawless area where groups of outlaws often ruled and the point of a gun was the only law.

At the point of a gun… Another good phrase he wanted to record.

He pushed through the batwing doors and saw a crowd of men in cowboy garb standing near a crudely fashioned bar. The walls were unpainted and the floor was made up of uneven, rough planks. Rows of dark bottles and haphazardly arranged glasses resided on shelves fashioned around a long mirror that ran behind the bar. Several tables and chairs occupied the expansive room, and three scantily clad barmaids made the rounds placing steins of beer and glasses of whiskey in front of customers. Leading the procession was a big, barrel-chested man in a blue shirt and black, leather vest. He wore no hat and his hair was long and tucked back, hanging over his collar. The hair was dark brown, but the man's beard was gray. His smile was broad as he placed some kind of ornaments, one by one, onto a straight, iron bar. As Buckner drew closer, he saw that the ornaments were, in fact, badges of some sort. Four five-pointed stars. There was some kind of inscription along the ridge, but Buckner wasn't close enough to read it.

Hot damn, he thought. This place is rich in material.

It was just the kind of place his editor back in New York had urged him to find.

"Go west, Buckner," his editor had said. "Go west and seek out the kind of characters we can put in our books. Strong, hard men. Gunfighter types, who would just as soon kill a man as look at him. That's the kind of stuff our readers want to read about. That's the kind of stuff that'll sell."

Buckner placed his traveling bag on the chair and dug out his notebook and a pencil. He absolutely had to get this down now.

"And here's the final one," the bearded man holding the badges said as he slipped the last one on the iron rod. Buckner was able to count five of them. The bearded man held the rod up for all to view, and then turned to an even bigger man standing to his left. Buckner could only see the back of the new man, but he was even taller than the other one. He had enormous shoulders and a black, Irish derby perched atop his head.

"All right, Finn," the bearded man said. "Show us how strong you are."

The huge man, turned and Buckner caught a glimpse of long, jet black hair, high cheekbones, with light blue eyes. The man's features had the look of an Indian, but his complexion was that of a white man. His lips peeled back exposing a set of crooked teeth.

As he reached for the rod, the bearded man leaned back suddenly.

"Hey, wait a minute," he said, staring at Buckner. "We got us a dude come to visit."

Buckner felt himself flush. He flashed a weak smile and removed his own hat.

"I beg your pardon, gentlemen," he said. "I didn't mean to disturb the festivities."

"You talk funny," one of the grubby cowboys said. "You a Yankee?"

"I just got here from New York, if that's what you mean."

"New York?" another cowboy said. "New York City?"

Buckner kept the smile on his lips and nodded. He was suddenly cognizant that although he was in the West, he was also south of the Mason/Dixon. "Well, I'm originally from Zanesville, Ohio," he added hastily.

"What you doin' here, dude?" the cowboy asked.

"Yeah, what you want?" demanded another.

Noticing that the crowd was turning a bit hostile, Buckner set his notebook and pencil down on the table and opened up his traveling bag. "Perhaps these will help explain." He took out several copies of the dime novels he'd brought with him and passed them around. "I'm a writer and I happen to be very interested in western culture, most specifically, men like yourselves."

He saw his words were being wasted as one grubby cowboy after another paged through the dime novels with perplexed look. It suddenly dawned on Buckner that the literacy rate among these creatures might not be too great.

"Lemme see one of them," the big, bearded man said. He set the iron rod with the badges on the bar.

One of the men passed him a book and said, "Here yah go, Burt."

The bearded man glared at the cowboy who'd handed him the book.

The cowboy balked and added, "I mean, Mr. McTavish."

The bearded man stared at the cowboy a few seconds more, and Buckner saw the fear dancing over the cowboy's face.

Was not calling a man by his surname a killing offense around these parts?

The bearded man, McTavish, transferred his gaze to the dime novel in front of him. The cover was colored with bright yellows and reds, brandishing the title of *JESSIE JAMES, KING OF THE OUTLAWS*.

Buckner suddenly wondered how the "outlaw" designation would be received by this crowd, but he felt it would be better than the books featuring Wild Bill Hickok. After all, he'd been a lawman at one time, and this group did not look particularly law abiding.

McTavish paged through the book, his eyebrows raising. The room grew silent. Buckner knew that this was a make-or-break moment. His whole future in Temptation would be decided in the next few moments. Would he be accepted, run out of town on a rail, or worse?

He sincerely hoped for the former.

McTavish looked up and grinned.

Buckner felt a little better, but the grin had a certain, malevolent quality to it. This was far from closed.

"You gonna make me as famous as Jessie?" McTavish asked.

Buckner's mouth was getting tired of having the smile frozen in place. He knew he had to choose his next words carefully. Very carefully.

"I'd certainly like to try," Buckner said, quickly adding,"Mr. McTavish."

That made the other man smile. He left his place at the bar and strode toward Buckner, who noticed how intimidating McTavish was up close. Twin pistols were housed in finely crafted leather holsters. He exuded strength and competence. There was no doubt he was the leader of this rag-tag band of misfits. McTavish stopped and leaned forward, his big, beardy face a few inches from Buckner's. The man's breath was very bad.

"Compared to me," he said, "Jessie James ain't nothing but a Missouri hill rat."

Buckner compressed his lips, then nodded.

"Runnin' and hidin'," McTavish said. "Shit, that's all him and his dumb brother do. Giving outlaws a bad name."

Buckner nodded again.

McTavish held the dime novel in front of Buckner's face, then flipped the book upward, toward the ceiling, which was rather high. The book flipped open at the apex, and fell to the floor in an unoccupied portion of the room. In a flash McTavish withdrew one of the pistols from its holster, cocked back the hammer, and fired.

The book skittered across the wooden floorboards

Buckner cast a furtive glance downward. He gulped. Was he next? The crowd was silent, or did it only seem so due to the ringing in Buckner's ears?

McTavish stared at him for a solid ten seconds, and then laughed.

Everyone else laughed, too.

McTavish holstered his gun, which made Buckner feel slightly better.

"Like I said..." McTavish spread his arms out in an expansive gesture. "All that dumb asshole Jessie does is hit and run. Us... We got us a whole damn town. You know what the lawmen say around these parts?"

Buckner shook his head.

The bearded man's lips curled back exposing yellowed teeth. "Lead us not into Temptation."

Buckner waited, and when McTavish laughed, so did everyone else. Buckner smiled, too, and reached for his notebook. "May I quote you on that, Mr. McTavish?"

McTavish leaned close again and whispered, "You damn well better."

With a laugh, he placed his arm around Buckner's shoulders and ushered him over to the bar. The iron rod still lay on top of it, and Buckner got close enough to read the inscription on the stars: *DEPUTY MARSHAL*. Two of the badges had bloody stains on them.

Good lord, Buckner thought. What have I gotten myself into?

"Lemme introduce you to some of my boys," McTavish said. He slapped a hand on the huge man's shoulder. "This here is the strongest man in these parts. Go ahead, Finn. Show the dude what you can do."

The big man swallowed the last bit of amber fluid in the glass in front of him and took the iron rod by each end, palms up. His face began to contort slightly.

Buckner suddenly realized that Finn was bending the iron rod. And he was making it look easy. The five badges jangled together in the center. He stopped when the ends of the bar met in an almost even circle.

McTavish grinned and slapped Finn on the shoulder again. He grabbed the iron circle and held it up for all to admire. A round of applause swept through the room. Buckner set his notebook down and clapped as well. He figured he'd not dare otherwise.

McTavish motioned for the bartender to take the iron circle and place it on a hooked nail on the wall next to the mirror. "Then set up another round, on the house."

As cowboys began to belly-up to the bar, Buckner picked up his notebook and began to scribble down the things he had seen.

"Your given name is Finn, sir?" he asked.

Before the big man could reply, McTavish interceded. "His given name's actually Wandering Buffalo. He's a breed. Half Cherokee, half Irish. The Indians didn't want him and the whites didn't, neither. But I do." McTavish smiled and looked at the big half-breed. "Which is why I give him that hat and renamed him Finnegan."

The big half-breed doffed the derby and grinned.

"And then there's Tom Mex," McTavish said to a man in a sombrero. "Or, Tomás, as he likes to be called."

The Mexican's white teeth flashed under his bushy mustache. "Best man with a knife I ever seen. Even better than Crow, here." McTavish leaned over and snatched the hat off the man hunched over a bottle and a glass on the bar. The man, whose head was devoid of hair and covered with a mass of red and purple scars, snarled a profanity, but made no move against McTavish, who laughed. "He was scalped a long time ago, but they didn't finish the job. Wanna know why?"

Buckner nodded.

"Cause I kilt 'em dead," the man named Crow said. "I kilt 'em all. Now gimme back my damn hat, please."

McTavish laughed again and slapped the hat back on Crow's head. "So now he spends his time doing scouting and tracking for me. In fact, he was just finishing up a little job."

"This is all so fascinating," Buckner said. "Totally fascinating." He scribbled in his notebook with his pencil. "The people back East are going to love it."

"They'd better, dude," McTavish said, leaning close enough that Buckner was once again reminded of how foul the man's breath smelled. "Otherwise, it ain't gonna get wrote. Understand?"

Buckner flashed the weak smile again and nodded. "Let me ask you one question, Mr. McTavish."

The bearded man lifted an eyebrow.

"Ah…" Buckner continued, "aren't you worried about the law?"

McTavish laughed and shook his head. "Not at all." He grabbed his vest and pulled it away from his shirt displaying a large, silver badge that said, *DEPUTY MARSHAL.*

Buckner's eyes widened and he smiled again and nodded. This was either going to be the biggest break of his career, or the one that broke him.

On the trail
The Indian Territories

Reeves rode on his big, dappled gray stallion so he could keep an eye on the five tethered horses he and Bear had secured to the back of the wagon. Without knowing who the owners of the stolen steeds were, Reeves figured he'd let Judge Parker determine what to do with them. More than likely, the judge would tell Reeves to keep the horses as part of his payment for bringing the Gunther boys to justice. Reeves actually regretted not being able to bring them back alive, which was both his and the judge's preference. But they'd left him little choice. The judge would understand. He knew Reeves was a man of his word.

The wide prairie began to narrow a bit as a series of grassy hills and clusters of trees began to crop up. The ground dipped into a long, sloping declivity and the trail wound toward a wide ravine of sorts, and Reeves immediately scanned the uppermost ridges on both sides.

Good place for an ambush.

He signaled Bear to hold up.

"See something?" Bear asked, pulling the reins to slow the team of horses to a stop.

"I'm gonna scout those ridges. Make sure nobody's up there."

Bear nodded. "Shoot if you need me to come in a hurry."

Reeves nodded and set off, urging his horse into a quick trot. As he moved along with the animal's loping gait, he let his forearm rest momentarily on the butt of one of his revolvers. The weapon's proximity gave him reassurance.

As he crested the top of the closest ridge, he saw no one. He slowed the horse to a walk and proceeded along, taking all the details into consideration.

"I'm gonna scout those ridges. Make sure nobody's up there."

No one was on either side, but the remnants of a sloppy camp—a long extinguished fire, a jury-rigged lean-to where they'd tied their horses, and some discarded tin cans, told him that someone had been up here in the recent past. But for what reason?

Ambush site, his gut told him.

With that, he dismounted and checked the detritus on the ground before him. The tops of the tin cans had apparently been cut open with a knife, then drained of their contents. He brought one of the cans to his nose.

Peaches.

That, and the sloppy disregard of the site told him it was white men, not Indians, in all probability. He walked over to the lean-to. These horses were shod. The tracks confirmed it. Definitely not Indians. He walked toward the edge and saw something else: a shell casing.

Stooping down, he picked it up and saw it was a .44-40 round from a Winchester rifle.

More shells littered the ground along the way toward the other end of the ridge—more .44-40's mixed with some .38-40's.

An ambush, all right. More than one or two men, from the looks of it. Way more. They'd tied their horses on the far side so as not to spook them too much when the firing started. It looked like the quarry was coming from the west. This was no hasty, pick-up ambush. It was planned. Well planned.

Reeves glanced at the opposite side. Something glittered in the hot, afternoon sun, and he assumed it was more shell casings. There'd been shooters on both sides. Thorough and deadly.

He looked downward and saw the bodies lying along the trail at the base of the gorge. Six men, shot down like pigs trapped in a poke.

They never had a chance, he thought.

Temptation City Saloon
The Indian Territories

Buckner watched as McTavish fondled the bargirl's full breast through the fabric of her dress. In his other hand, he held a dime novel.

"Turn the page for me, honey," McTavish said.

The girl giggled and flipped the page over.

Her teeth, Buckner noticed, were dreadful. Other than that, she wasn't bad looking, if you could get past the musky smell and the tuffs of blond hair sprouting from her armpits. He hadn't taken a bath in over a week, and he was certain that it had been much longer in her case.

This one-horse town could use the services of a public bathhouse and a good dentist, he thought.

But still, when he wrote about her, he was going to have to use a bit of artistic license. Make her more attractive. Perhaps she did have some redeeming features. Not that he'd been tempted to sample her wares to gain more insight. Her bad teeth and foul body odor repulsed him. Plus, all of the bar girls seemed to be spoken for by the members of McTavish's gang, and Buckner had no desire to get on the wrong side of any of those gunmen. Despite McTavish claiming to be the marshal, these men were obviously all ruthless outlaws. Buckner hoped he could gather enough material, soak up enough setting, listen to their stories, to be able to write several books. The trick was to make McTavish think the work would lionize him, but that probably wouldn't be too difficult.

He watched the big man's brow furrow as his lips moved over the words. From the look of it, McTavish could barely decipher the words. He was no more than an oversized dummy with a pair of guns. But he was definitely a dangerous, oversized dummy, too.

The reality was that although Buckner was fascinated by the brutal nature of these men, their rugged lifestyle fascinated him. If he could capture the essence of their savagery, perhaps it wouldn't be necessary to depict them as heroes.

McTavish laughed and flipped the book closed. "I gotta hand it to you, dude. You know how to tell a story."

Buckner smiled. "Thank you, Mr. McTavish."

"Ah, call me Burt." He tossed the book onto the table and placed both hands on the girl's breasts. "I think I'd like the title of Bad Burt McTavish. Whaddaya think?"

Buckner nodded vigorously. "Has a ring to it."

"A ring?"

"Ah... a ring, as in felicitous sound to the phrasing."

McTavish frowned, his voice a low growl: "I don't like it much when you use them big words."

"Sorry," Buckner said, trying to swallow the lump in his throat. "I only meant..."

"Never mind that." McTavish grabbed the girl by the waist and lifted her off his lap. "Polly, go fetch me a drink."

She smiled and sashayed toward the bar. McTavish reached out and swatted her on the ass, causing her to smile and show those bad teeth again.

"She's quite a gal," McTavish said.

"I'll bet."

The outlaw grinned slightly. "Want to get a little taste? I'll have her take you upstairs for some fun. I guarantee she'll curl your toes."

Buckner flashed a quick smile. The idea almost made him nauseous. "But... I thought she was your girl?"

"My girl? Polly?" McTavish laughed and shook his head. "Not hardly. She's just something to pass the time on dull afternoon... Or night. She does come in handy, though. Especially when them blue bellies come out this way."

"Blue bellies?" Buckner asked.

"Cavalry soldiers. From Fort Carson, a ways west. They still patrol out this aways, even though the Injun problems are pretty much done with 'round here. Mostly, they keep an eye on the railroad when there's something important coming through." He took a crudely wrapped cigar from his pocket. "Yeah, Polly does come in handy. Them blue bellies like to talk after they done it with her. Braggin' mostly, but every once in a while something good comes out of it." McTavish dipped both ends of the cigar into his mouth, licking and smoothing the leaves, then placed it between his lips. Taking a large, wooden match from his vest pocket, he flicked his thumbnail across the primer end, lighting it, and then held it to the end of the cigar and leaned closer to Buckner. "Bad Burt..." McTavish drew in several copious puffs. "I want to be bigger than Jessie James, understand?"

The cloud of smoke almost made Buckner choke, but he nodded. "I'm sure you will be, with the right approach."

"Approach? What you mean by that?"

Buckner felt a shiver of fear traverse his spine. He was sure to end up in a shallow grave if he said the wrong thing and got on this big brute's wrong side. "I just meant to say that Jessie James had the advantage of being first, that's all."

McTavish just stared at him, the air between them a grayish haze.

"I mean," Buckner continued, "James was cast as sort of a hero after defending those settlers against the railroad. It made him look like a defender of the common man."

"Sheeit," McTavish said. "He ain't nothing but Missouri hill trash. Look how him and his gang messed up that bank robbery in that place up north." He drew on the cigar, causing the tip to glow red.

"Northfield, Minnesota," Buckner said. "I'm surprised you know about that one."

McTavish sat up straight and stared at him, blowing a thin stream of smoke out of the side of his mouth.

Buckner sensed that he'd said the wrong thing and swallowed hard.

Polly came back with another shot glass filled with whiskey. McTavish grabbed the glass from her and tossed the drink down. "Bring me the bottle and another glass."

She snickered again and left. McTavish leaned forward. "Dude, you and me gonna have a little drink, and a little talk. It's time you learned I ain't as dumb as you think."

"I… I…. I never thought that."

McTavish grinned. "You'd best not." The girl returned with the bottle and McTavish poured a drink for himself and one for Buckner. He shoved the glass forward. Buckner had little choice but to accept it.

"Buckner, huh?" McTavish said, lifting the glass and marveling at the amber liquid. "What you say your first name was?"

"Julian. Julian Henry Buckner, the Third."

"The third?" McTavish's laugh was low and guttural. "You got enough names for two men. How 'bouts I just call you Julia?"

"Ah, it's *Jew-lee-an*," Buckner said, drawing out the pronunciation.

"Okay, Julia," McTavish said with a wry grin, puffing on the cigar again. "Drink up."

They raised the glasses and Buckner felt the awful, hot burn of the worst alcohol he'd ever tasted. He coughed for several seconds and McTavish laughed.

"I got something planned that's gonna make Jessie James look like a schoolboy throwing rocks at a buildin'," McTavish said, his words enveloped in a cloudy breath. "After that, I'm gonna be a rich man. Buy myself a nice spread down Mexico way, and raise me a whole passel of cattle."

Buckner was still feeling the effects of the rot gut whiskey. When he spoke, his voice sounded almost falsetto "I'd be interested in hearing more about it."

McTavish smirked and poured himself another drink, then held the bottle toward Buckner, who shook his head. McTavish shrugged, then asked, "Question is, Julia, can I trust you?"

"Of course you can." Buckner's voice had returned to normal.

McTavish blew out more smoke, then dropped the cigar on the floor. The toe of his boot ground it to pulp as he said, "I'd better be able to, Dude." His right hand dropped to his boot and came up with a mean-looking knife which he held under Buckner's chin. "Otherwise, I'll cut yer throat and drop you down the hole in the shithouse. Understand?"

Buckner tried to nod and felt the point of the knife scratch his chin. "Absolutely, Mr. McTavish," he said, without moving his head again.

McTavish smiled. "Julia, I thought I told you to start calling me Burt?"

The Indian Territories

"**T**his one's still alive," Bear said, kneeling next the sixth man. "Barely."

Reeves had finished checking the others…all shot dead. That one was still breathing was a miracle in itself. He grabbed his canteen and trotted over to Bear. The Indian looked up at him and shook his head slightly.

Reeves nodded and knelt next to the fallen man, using his own body to shield him from the blazing sun, and bathed his face with some water from his canteen.

The man's eyes opened and he looked up "Who are yah?" His voice was a husky rasp.

"I'm a lawman." Reeves held the canteen to the man's lips and allowed him a small drink.

The man's lips twitched into something that might have been intended to be a smile. Reeves could tell the man was close to death "Lawman?" He swallowed hard, then coughed. "A Negro?"

Reeves nodded. "A free man and a lawman."

"Look, I ain't got much time left. Promise me you'll bury us all so the buzzards won't finish us off."

"We'll bury anybody that needs burying," Reeves said. "You take it easy. Who done this to you?"

The man tried to swallow again.

Reeves held his canteen to the man's lips again to give him another small sip.

The man nodded a thanks and asked, "You really a lawman?"

Reeves held his vest open, displaying his deputy marshal badge.

The man nodded. "Reckon you are." His left hand moved to the blood-stained dirt and his fingers dug back and forth. Something silver glinted in the sun. The man coughed wetly; blood splattered the ground by his mouth.

"Let me do that," Reeves said.

He took out his knife and shoved the blade into the earth, then pried out a silver star, surrounded by a circular rim, upon which was the inscription, *Deputy Marshal*.

"You a marshal?" Reeves asked.

The man nodded. "Name's Frank Moore. We came outta Texas following the McTavish gang. They been sellin' guns and whiskey to the Injuns. Causin' lots of trouble."

"What tribe?" Reeves asked.

"Comanches mostly." Moore coughed again. "They been stealing the government-issued cattle from the Injuns, too. Stirring up lots of trouble. We took to callin' 'em White Comanches. Comancheros."

Reeves had heard the name. Outlaws intent on causing havoc between the Indians and the settlers.

"We was following a man named Crow," Moore said. "Supposed to lead us to McTavish's gang." He paused and coughed again. Another spot of blood spattered his chin. Reeves wiped it off.

"Crow was scalped by Injuns," the man said. "Said it made him want to help us." His lips twisted into a frown. "Damn bastard was lying the whole time. Led us into an ambush. 'Fore we knew what happened, they opened fire from up on the ridge." His eyes closed. "Shot us all to hell, stole our horses."

"Your horses?"

The man nodded. "Then the bastards picked through the bodies, stole our stars, too. I managed to push mine into the dirt and cover it over before I passed out. Couldn't move my gun arm, or I'd have taken one or two of them with me."

"Take it easy, Marshal," Reeves said. "We got us a wagon. We'll get you to a doc."

Moore's smile was wistful. He shook his head. "Too late. Just bury me with them."

He coughed again and more color drained from his face. Reeves figured the man had only a few minutes left. "If you could send my star back to my kin folk, I'd be obliged, Marshal."

Reeves said he would, and Moore recited the mailing address.

Reeves didn't mention that neither he nor Bear could read or write. Instead, Reeves committed it to memory, hoping he'd be able to remember it completely by the time he got back to Fort Smith, so Judge Parker could write it down for him.

"I'll do my best to make sure it gets there," Reeves said. "And I'll get the rest of them stars back, too. I pledge to you that I'll track down your killers and bring them in for what they done."

"I'm obliged to you, Marshal." Moore closed his eyes and shook as he expelled his last breath.

Reeves and Bear placed the six bodies into the wagon and moved them out of the gulley to a shady spot near a cluster of trees. It looked to be an appropriate resting place, and the two men set about burying the fallen lawmen. Several hours later, both covered in sweat, Reeves and Bear stood in front of the six covered graves. Reeves thought about placing a cross on each one, but instead left them unmarked. There were too many renegades in the Territories who would desecrate a gravesite in hopes of finding something of value; a ring, a watch, or even some gold in the corpse's teeth. Instead, Reeves carefully transplanted a cluster of wild flowers to the recently disturbed earth, hoping that the flowers would flourish and form a natural marker.

He removed his hat and bowed his head. Bear stood beside him watching.

"Don't know the right words to say," Reeves said, "but my mama used to be fond of the twenty-third psalm. Yay, though I walk through the valley of death, I shall fear no evil, for your rod and your staff comfort me."

After Reeves had completed his recitation of the passage, Bear said. "May the Great Spirit watch over them."

Reeves nodded, whispered a prayer over the graves, and silently reaffirmed the pledge that he would do his best to bring the outlaws who'd done this to justice.

"What now?" Bear asked, wiping away the sweat that had collected on his headband.

Reeves took out his handkerchief and wiped his own face, pondering their next move. The lawmen had obviously been led into a death trap by the man known as Crow. They'd been after the McTavish gang, so it was a safe bet that this McTavish was behind the ambush. It had occurred in the Indian Territories, and Reeves had given his word that the men responsible would be brought to justice. He pointed to the trail.

"Let's see what the tracks tell us."

He and Bear moved over to the flat area and began scouring the ground. After about thirty seconds of looking, Bear grunted.

"Got some here."

Reeves joined him and studied the impressions and the surrounding area for a solid minute.

"I'd say at least ten riders," Reeves said. "What you make outta these tracks here?"

Bear walked over and stared downward, moving his head slowly from right to left.

"Looks like some of them horses had no riders," he said.

Reeves nodded. "Just what I was thinking. Remember, Moore said the gang took their stars and their horses. Question is, why?"

Bear shrugged. "To sell?"

"Maybe. We need to find out a bit more about this McTavish and his gang."

"We gonna bring 'em in, Dark Panther?"

"If you gonna keep callin' me that, I just might make up a new name for y'all."

Bear grinned. "I told you, in the tongue of my people it is a name of respect."

Reeves chuckled. He'd ridden with Bear numerous times on these long chases, and the man's sense of humor always made things interesting. "Yeah, well, maybe I will think up a new name for you. Something like Walks in Bear Dung."

"Hey," the Indian raised an eyebrow and looked insulted. "I told you, Indians take our names very seriously.

Reeves slung the shovel onto his massive shoulder, turned, and walked back toward the wagon and their horses. "Yeah, well, the white men we tracking probably have a couple of names for both of us that we'll be hearin' soon enough that ain't related to either respect or honor."

Bear held his shovel by the middle of the handle and followed.

Horse Stables, Temptation City

"**J**ulia," McTavish said, ushering Buckner inside the darkened interior of the large stable. The windows had been boarded over, but slits of the fading afternoon sunlight filtered in through the unevenly placed planks illuminating the agitated dust motes. "This is what's gonna separate me from that little piker, Jessie James." He tapped his index finger on the side of his head. "I got me the plan of all plans."

Buckner had a grin plastered on his face, but his stomach was still roiling from the rot gut. He wondered if he went into the corner to vomit, would it offend McTavish? It felt like the so-called whiskey had permanently seared his throat.

McTavish closed the door behind them and grabbed a lantern. Lifting the glass, he pulled out a big, wooden match and flicked it with his thumbnail. The nearest horses whined with discomfort or fear, Buckner wasn't sure which. The stable was filled with the animals; at least twenty of them.

McTavish chuckled and lighted the wick, then lowered the glass. "Over here."

They walked in the dark interior toward the rear stalls. It was a huge place and Buckner caught a glimpse of three large wagons off in the corner. Each one had a dirty tan canvas covering over its bed. The yokes looked they were designed for four horses.

McTavish strode toward them and stopped. He held the lantern up, leaned over, and glanced around. Buckner couldn't see what McTavish was looking at, but when he turned back around, he had a broad smile on this face. He reached in his pocket and took out a long, crumpled cigar and placed it between his lips.

Buckner expected the outlaw to light it, but he didn't. He just stood there smiling, like a proud papa.

The remnants of the rot gut were still eating at Buckner's stomach. He wanted nothing more than to go back to his room at the hotel and lie down.

McTavish rolled the cigar between his lips, but still didn't light it.

Canting his head to one side, he said, "Remember I told you Polly gets real friendly with them cavalry soldiers?"

Buckner nodded. The thought of unwashed Polly's amorous activities on her featherbed made him more nauseous.

"Well," McTavish said, "like I told you, them blue bellies like to brag about how important they think they are. One of 'em let it slip that they'd be coming back this way in a couple-three days. Gonna be guardin' something big on that train from Denver to Fort Smith."

"Something big?"

McTavish's eyes narrowed for a moment, then he said one word with a hushed reverence: "Gold."

"Gold?"

McTavish nodded. "Yep. Gold. Lots of it. Upwards of twenty thousand dollars' worth."

Even in the lantern light, Buckner could see the look of rapture on the big outlaw's face.

On the trail
The Indian Territories

The tracks led toward Temptation, with no attempt at concealment or misdirection. As they drew nearer to the town, Reeves signaled Bear to come to a halt.

"You know anything about this town up ahead?" Reeves asked.

Bear shook his head. "Not much. Supposed to be a wild place."

Reeves grinned. "Ain't they all 'round here?"

Bear smiled back. "I also heard they don't like your kind much. Mine neither."

Reeves took off his hat and wiped the sweat off his forehead with his shirt sleeve. It was nearly dusk and the town was perhaps a mile or two away.

"Where are the nearest Lighthorses at?" Reeves asked.

Bear shrugged. "How the hell would I know?"

Reeves frowned. Bear had a point. The Lighthorses, of which Bear was one, were the Indian mounted police unit, and they were spread pretty thin. They only had jurisdiction over Indians, so it stood to reason they would be giving this place called Temptation a wide berth.

"What about the closest Indian village?" Reeves asked.

Bear smiled. "That, I do know." He pointed south.

"How far?"

"Maybe an hour's ride."

"Yep. Gold. Lots of it. Upwards of twenty thousand dollars' worth."

Reeves replaced his hat on his head and motioned Bear to turn the wagon and head south.

"Let's go pay 'em a visit," Reeves said. "We're gonna need a place to stash our horses and the wagon."

"What makes you think we can trust 'em?" Bear said with a grin. "You know how us redskins steal."

"Maybe we can find a couple of Lighthorses to go after 'em if they do."

Bear laughed. "That'll be the day."

Cherokee Village
The Indian Territories

As they rode into the small village Reeves took note that the only young males he saw were working a in a blighted swath of corn. Most of them looked barely past ten or eleven. A few smaller children ran up and eyed them with hungry, empty eyes. They were hustled away by a group of squaws. Bear said something to one of the women and she pointed to a teepee at the end of the encampment. An old man sat in front of it smoking a pipe.

"That's the tribal chief," Bear said.

"I gathered that." Reeves could speak several Indian languages, and had a working knowledge of Cherokee, but he could only decipher a few words of this dialect.

Bear halted the horses and set the brake. Reeves dismounted and tied the reins of his horse to the wagon. They approached the old Indian together. He did not acknowledge their presence until Bear squatted down in front of him. Reeves glanced around the camp and saw it was in pitiful condition. He joined Bear and also squatted down to be on eye level with the old Indian.

Bear and the old man were already in conversation. Reeves could follow a few words here and there.

Bear turned to him. "He asks if we have come about the missing beef?"

"Missing beef?"

Bear nodded. "Part of the treaty. After they killed all buffalo, the government promised to provide beef to keep the tribes from venturing out and rustling." He smirked. "And you know how good the government is at keeping its promises."

"Forty acres and a mule," Reeves said. He felt a twinge of kinship with the Indians and wasn't surprised. Both races had been trampled on and lied to by the white man and his government.

"Where are all the young braves?" Reeves asked.

Bear translated the question and the old Indian's mouth twisted downward. When he spoke, his voice sounded brittle.

"He says many died on the Trail of Tears. Others have left," Bear said. "Vanished. There is no hunting here, no food, except what they manage to grow. Many have been destroyed by the firewater the whites sell to them."

"Sell?" Reeves asked.

"They traded their government-issued beef for the whiskey," Bear said. "Until all the cows were gone, and then they didn't come back. Many of the young men left, too."

"Sad," Reeves said, thinking of his own time as a slave: no hope, no future. Fortunately, things had changed for him. These Indians weren't so lucky.

"What can he tell us about the town?" Reeves asked.

Bear and the chief spoke for several minutes. Reeves could understand a few phrases, which he interpreted as terms of disgust. When the old man finished speaking, he put the pipe back in his mouth and resumed his stoic posture.

"He calls it a pit of snakes," Bear said. "First came the white man's iron horse, the railroad. That destroyed the buffalo. Then white men started to build the town as a stop for the railroad, but never finished. The tracks now go past the town now to the fort where the white soldiers live. It's about a half day's ride from the town."

"So the place became a gathering place for outlaws," Reeves said. He'd surmised as much. It was an all-too-common pattern in the Territories. "Does he know anything about the men who live there now?"

Bear repeated the question. The old Indian removed the pipe from his mouth and spoke again.

"They are without honor," Bear said. "He has heard the group there now killed the sheriff and took over the town. There are some decent people who cower in fear in their houses and stores, but they are few now."

"He ever heard of a man called Crow?"

The old Indian's face twitched at the name. He spat out a response that Reeves understood without the translation, but he let Bear tell him anyway.

"Crow is no warrior," Bear said. "He is a coward. He hates the Indian because he was once scalped by the Creeks for trying to rape a child. He is one of the evil white tribe that lives there now."

Reeves considered their options, and decided they needed a base of operations. This was the logical spot. "Ask him for permission to camp here tonight and to leave our horses and wagon here for a day or two more. Tell him we'll pay."

Bear nodded and spoke to the old man. He nodded and replied in what Reeves took to be an ascent.

"He says we can do that," Bear said.

Reeves reached into his pocket and felt for his supply of silver dollars. He carried them as a reward to give to people who helped him. He had six left. Removing five, he handed them to the Bear and motioned him to give the coins to the old Indian.

The chief glanced at the glittering silver coins and shook his head, mumbling something again in the dialect.

"He says he does not want the white man's money," Bear said.

Reeves chuckled and extended his hands, pinching the flesh on the back of his left between his right thumb and forefinger. "I ain't no white man."

Bear smirked, translated.

The old Indian's lips parted in a slight smile. He picked up one of the coins, looked at it, and began speaking. Bear translated.

"He says it has great beauty. On one side, there is the eagle, and on the other, the face of a woman. He wonders if this will bring him luck on finding a new wife."

Reeves laughed. "Can't help him with that."

"He also says he would like two of your horses instead," Bear said.

Reeves shook his head. "I need mine and the ones for the wagon. As far as the others, they ain't mine to give. Got to turn 'em over to Judge Parker."

Bear translated and the old Indian nodded.

"Tell him he's welcome to our supply of extra food," Reeves said. "But warn him not to take it all. We might be bringin' back a few prisoners when we leave."

Bear translated again. The old Indian said something and then looked at Reeves.

"He says he senses that you are a great warrior," Bear said. "He thanks you for the food, and the coin. He will ask the Great Spirit to watch over you and me in our quest."

"Tell him thanks," Reeves said, standing up and placing the other four silver dollars in front of the old Indian. "I got a feeling we gonna need all the help we can get."

Temptation City

"That's a lot of gold," Buckner said as he followed McTavish through the stables toward the rear door.

The big, beardy outlaw glanced back over his shoulder at the dime novelist and grinned. "You're damn right it is."

Buckner swallowed, his stomach still roiling, the swirling inebriation now affecting his judgment. Otherwise, he hardly would have said, "Pardon me for playing the devil's advocate, Mr. McTavish, but…"

"Burt."

"No, but…"

"Burt, dammit," McTavish said. "I already done told you to call me Burt."

"Oh." Buckner could feel the whiskey's effects. He couldn't remember feeling so drunk so fast. Of course, he hadn't eaten all day.

"Now what was you saying?"

Buckner swallowed hard, wishing he had a crust of bread to gobble down. He blinked twice, trying to clear his head and formulate his next question so it wouldn't offend the big outlaw. Buckner desperately wanted to get the plan straight for the sake of his story, and what a story it would be… He'd be famous.

"I'm a talkin' to you, Julia," McTavish said. His voice was a low growl.

Buckner forced all the fanciful thoughts out of his head and smiled, realizing that it probably looked more like a simper at this point. "What was I saying?" He started to speak, but the roiling suddenly reached a critical point and he felt the vile liquid surging upward. Holding his gut, he ran to the corner, bent over, and threw up.

When he stood up and wiped his mouth, he saw McTavish chuckling. "Can't hold your liquor too good, huh, Julia?"

"It's just that… ah, I haven't eaten yet today."

McTavish grunted a laugh and unbuttoned his fly. "Well, I got to get rid of some of that whiskey, too. But from the other end." He turned and began urinating on the support post.

"Should you be doing that in here?" Buckner asked. A second later he realized there was still a sufficient amount of liquor in his system to override his better judgment.

McTavish was finishing up. "Ah, ain't like nobody's likely to notice with all the horse shit. You got some on your shoes, by the way."

Buckner glanced done and saw the smears from toe to spats. He tried to bend down to wipe it off, but then realized that would just get it on his fingers. He straightened up.

"Now what was you sayin' about the devil?" McTavish asked.

"The devil?" Buckner blinked again, his faculties slowed, but not dimmed. At least he didn't think so. "Oh, yes. That's a lot of gold. How will you transport it? I mean, if they're using a train…"

McTavish held the lantern higher and pointed with his free hand. His gun hand, Buckner noticed. "See them wagons there?"

Buckner looked. He remembered seeing the three huge vessels when they'd come in. He managed a nod.

"Well, I figure between the three of them, I'll have enough space. I got me an extra supply of horses, too," McTavish said. "Thanks in part to them Deputy Marshals." He emitted a low chuckle.

Buckner smiled reflexively. "But didn't you say there will be soldiers on the train?"

McTavish frowned. "So?"

"Well, I mean, aren't you afraid that they'll…" He searched for the right way to phrase it.

"Sheeeit. Didn't I tell you, I got this all planned out?"

Buckner managed to nod. Words were eluding him now.

McTavish motioned with his head for the dime novelist to follow. They went out the rear door and toward a shed about thirty feet away. The door had been chained shut and another wagon, a slightly smaller version, was parked next to it.

McTavish worked his fingers into his pants pocket and withdrew a key, which he stuck in the lock securing the chains on the shed door. The lock popped open and McTavish pulled the chain out of the hasps on the doors. The big man turned to face Buckner.

"This here's why I ain't afraid of no blue bellies," he said, and stepped back. When he pulled open the doors, Buckner struggled again to find the right words.

"Is that…" He blinked again, trying to formulate a sentence.

McTavish chuckled again, and this time Buckner felt it had a more sinister sound to it.

"Is that what I think it is?" Buckner asked, finally finding the words.
"It's called a Bulldog."

Temptation City

Reeves rode into Temptation on one of the horses they'd taken from the Gunther brothers. He'd picked this mount to match his disguise: a rather bedraggled looking cowboy who looked to be one step ahead of the law. Reeves had chosen a soiled, ripped shirt he kept in a burlap bag in his wagon. His pants were equally filthy, and the leather of the boots he wore was barely attached to the soles. He had many different disguises he used, from a preacher to an itinerate cowpoke, but figured this one would work the best in the lawless town he saw stretching out before him. It wasn't much. On the way into the town he'd noticed a set of dead-end railroad tracks. Apparently the railroad had once intended this place to be a regular stop on the way east or west, but that plan had long since been discarded. Foot-high weeds now sprouted up between the stone gravel and railroad ties. Reeves rode past a bunch of dilapidated wooden buildings ranging from a few stores, stables, and what appeared to be a saloon. A bigger, two-story building that looked like a hotel was across from the saloon next to a brick building Reeves assumed was a bank. It looked deserted, which didn't surprise him. From what the old Indian had told them, virtually all the decent people had been driven out of town a long time ago.

Deliver us not into Temptation, Reeves thought as he rode up to the saloon and stopped.

He'd told Bear to come in from the opposite side, the one closest to the Indian camp. Bear had taken the other Gunther horse, but Reeves instructed him to stash the horse so he could meander into Temptation on foot, disguised as a drunken Indian. Bear had reacted to the plan with his customary, ironic comment: "Unfortunately, around these parts it seems there ain't no other kind."

Reeves stared through the opening above the bat-wing doors. The place was crowded and it was barely past noon. Obviously, these guys wouldn't know an honest day's work if it rode up and bit them on the ass. He dismounted and wrapped the reins around the hitching post. As he pushed through the doors at least a dozen sets of hostile eyes regarded him. Reeves regretted that he'd taken only one of his Colt .45 Peacemakers, figuring that a man with two of those guns in twin holsters might look too affluent. He did have the gun Gunther had given him tucked in the side of his belt. A big man with a grayish beard and a black, leather vest leaned with his back against the bar while a bunch of other seedy looking cowboys sat around him with expressions of adoration.

The king holding court, Reeves thought. Most like, he's McTavish.

A dude in a fancy suit sat at the closest table scribbling with a pencil on a piece of paper. A giant stood on the other side of the bearded man. The giant wore a fancy, round hat, and had the facial bones of an Indian, but his skin and eyes were light.

Half-breed, Reeves thought.

Something else caught his eye: a metal ring with five lawman stars hung above the bar. This was most likely the right place.

"Finnegan is the only man strong enough to lift it," the bearded man was saying. "Can pick it up and turn it like a toy. And Tom Mex is fast enough on his feet to keep up with the cranking."

Reeves pushed through the doors and the bearded man stopped talking. All the eyes in the place turned to stare.

"Hey, nigger," the fat man behind the bar said. "We don't serve your kind here. You see the sign?"

Reeves didn't let the words bother him. He'd been called worse. And he also knew he had to remain faithful to the role he was playing; a man down on his luck and on the run.

"I never could do no readin' or writin'," Reeves said. The bartender reached down behind the bar and came up with a Parker shotgun. Reeves pulled his Peacemaker out of his holster and held it down by his leg, cocking back the hammer. Playing a role was one thing. Reeves wasn't about to get shot by some race-hating cracker.

"Hey, Henry," the big man with a beard said, stepping forward. Reeves caught a glimpse of a star on the man's shirt, partially hidden behind his leather vest. "No need for that scattergun." He looked Reeves up and down, then grinned. "You look like you got somebody on your ass, boy. That right?"

Reeves watched as the cracker bartender placed the shotgun back under the bar. He made a mental note to remember it was there, in the likely event that he'd be making a return visit. He eased down the hammer and replaced the Colt in its holster.

"Let's just say, sir," Reeves said, feigning deference, "that I been riding hard for three days. I sure could use a plate of beans, if'n' you got some to spare, sir."

The big man smirked. "We look like a charity outfit? You got money?"

Reeves shook his head. "None to speak of, but I be glad to trade a gun for a good meal."

"Gun?" The bearded man's left eyebrow arched upward. "What kinda gun?"

Reeves licked his lips, still playing his role of a nervous, down-on-his-luck cowpoke. He gingerly withdrew the revolver that he'd taken from Gunther and set it on the bar.

The bearded man motioned for the gun to be pushed toward him.

"What kind is it?" he asked.

"It's a Remington, sir," Reeves said, giving the gun a shove.

"Is that a good one, Burt?" the dude sitting at the table asked.

The bearded man glared down at him, like he was deciding whether or not to slap him. He picked up the Remington and immediately checked the cylinder.

"It's empty."

"Yes, sir," Reeves said. "But I do have some extra cartridges."

The bearded man hefted the gun in his fist, cocking back the hammer and checking the weapon's action. He lowered the hammer, then cocked it back again, repeating this several times.

The man knows how to handle a gun, Reeves thought. He waited.

"Henry," the bearded man said, "give the boy here a plate of your beans and glass of beer." He glared toward Reeves. "You take it outside, boy, and don't leave without givin' me them cartridges."

Reeves nodded. He'd seen all he needed to see: fifteen heavily armed, hardened men... Outlaws... Killers... Bushwackers, every last one of them, except maybe for that slicked-up dude.

The bartender, Henry, called out and a girl in a lace dress popped her head out of the door by the back.

"Give this nigger a plate of beans and a beer," Henry said, and turned back to Reeves with a scowl.

Reeves stood waiting. The girl came waltzing into the main room with a plate overflowing with reddish beans in one hand and a stein of beer in the other.

"Throw them away after he's done," Henry said. "Don't bother washin' 'em."

Reeves thought that he was going to enjoy knocking that fat asshole down a peg or two, if and when the time came. For now, though, he had to wait. He accepted the plate and beer and started toward the doors, when they flew open and Bear fell through, his hands gripping a rope around his neck.

"Move, *chingado*," a Mexican in a large *sombrero* said from behind Bear. The Mex held the rope, walking Bear like a dog on a leash. "Hey, *patron*, look what I find sneaking around down by the stables."

The Mex forced Bear down on his knees in the middle of the floor. Reeves stood in place, waiting to see how this would play out. The Mexican pulled out a knife and held it against Bear's neck. The tip dug into skin, causing a thread of crimson to spill downward.

"That right, chief?" the bearded man asked. "You snoopin' 'round where you don't belong?"

Bear gasped, seemingly unable to speak.

Reeves figured if things got worse, he'd shoot the Mexican first, then the bearded man second. After that, he probably wouldn't be around to fire a third time.

"Answer the man, *chingado*," the Mex said, digging the point of the knife in deeper. The blood flow increased, but wound still looked minor.

"You got firewater?" Bear croaked. "Me lookin' for firewater. Me clean 'em horses. Good job. Gimme firewater."

"You like shovelin' horseshit?" the bearded man said with a smile. His face dropped all signs of mirth. "Let him go, Tomás."

The Mexican's face took on a sour expression. "Aww, *heeell*." He withdrew the knife and slipped it back into a sheath on his belt.

Reeves took notice of the knife's location. The Mexican looked like he knew how to use it.

"I said let him go," the bearded man said. "We don't need no Injun agents nosing around here with our plan about to…" He stopped talking and glared at Reeves, and then Bear. "Just get 'em outta here."

"Lemme scalp him first," another man said. He leaned forward and Reeves saw that the man's head was a mass of scars.

"Aww, shut up, Crow," McTavish said. "Just cause you ain't got no more hair's no reason to deprive somebody else of their's."

Crow, Reeves thought. The man who'd led the lawmen into the ambush. He took note of the man's face. He'd be one to remember.

The Mexican's lips bunched together, but he loosened the rope. Bear pulled it from around his neck and ducked his head free. For a moment

Reeves worried that Bear would turn around and hit the Mexican. Reeves wouldn't blame him. If the role had been reversed, Reeves would have knocked the bastard into the bone orchard.

But Bear caught Reeves's eye and he knew that his partner was all right. He kept to his role as the drunken Indian. Bear began scurrying toward the doors. The Mexican kicked him hard on the ass.

"*Salga, mierdra,*" the Mex said.

"Are Indian agents a problem around here, Burt?" the dude asked, his pencil poised over the paper.

The bearded man shot him an angry look and shook his head, then turned back to the Mexican. "Just let the damn Injun go." He then looked at Reeves again. "And you, get the hell outta here, too, boy."

Reeves nodded and followed Bear out the doors. When they were both outside and Reeves estimated that they were out of earshot he whispered to Bear, asking if he was all right. The Indian nodded fractionally and kept rubbing his neck. He usually wore his hair tied up in a braid behind his head, but for this disguise he'd let it fall around his shoulders. It gave him a wild look.

"You hear what that stinkin' Mex called me?" he said, his voice hoarse. "*Mierdra.*"

"Means shit in Spanish," Reeves said. He had a working knowledge of that language as well.

"I owe that bastard one," Bear whispered back. "When the time comes, he's mine."

Reeves nodded and said, "Meet you back at camp."

Bear cast Reeves a knowing wink and staggered away in the direction of the stables. Reeves figured his partner had stashed his horse somewhere in that direction. Squatting down, Reeves quickly ate the beans and drank a few swallows of beer. It was warm and flat.

A rider came galloping in from the west, his horse lathered up from the pace. He pulled the animal to a halt and jumped off, wrapping the reins around the hitching rail and literally ran through the batwing doors.

"Mr. McTavish," the rider, who was as lathered up as his horse, yelled as he entered. "I got some news. They already done left early from Denver."

Reeves remained where he was, straining his ears to hear more, but all he heard was McTavish's growl.

"Quit yer hollerin', you God damn idiot." The growl was followed by the sound of a meaty slap and yelp of pain.

Reeves had finished the beans. Bear had disappeared from the dusty street, and Reeves knew it was time for him to take his leave as well. For now, anyway.

He took one more sip and worked the liquid around in his mouth before spitting it out. Glancing back through the doors, Reeves took one more look inside.

There was more to be learned here, but not with this masquerade. He had a different tactic in mind.

Temptation City Hotel

Buckner struggled to keep his stomach contents under control as he made his way up the dimly lighted stairs to his hotel room. It was close to midnight and he had a very important appointment in the morning. McTavish had insisted on Buckner downing more of the rot gut whiskey as they sat at a corner table and McTavish laid out the way he wanted to be portrayed in the dime novel.

"Remember," the repulsive oaf had said, "I wanna be bigger than Jessie James. Bad Burt's gonna be a legend 'cause I got more smarts than him, too. I got me a foolproof plan."

Buckner had smiled and guzzled his way through the conversation, scribbling down as many notes as he could. In truth, he was more than a little bothered by the details: the killing of all those soldiers... more than twenty of them, was troubling. But, if he was completely honest with himself, it was also a tad exciting. Not that he condoned McTavish's plan for the robbery and slaughter, but the chance to view the event up close, to actually be there, took his breath away. Buckner had been too young to fight in the War, but one of his uncles had. He seldom talked about what he saw or did, but once mentioned that he'd seen a lot of men die. As a young boy, Buckner had asked him what it was like, but his uncle shook his head and said he couldn't find the words to describe it. Buckner hoped he could. He'd dreamed of writing a novel about the conflict, one that would be hailed as a masterpiece. But instead, he was writing dime novels that merged fact with fiction, made heroes of killers. Still, the chance to see this kind of thing for himself was the chance of a lifetime.

He managed to climb that last stair and paused at the top, gripping the banister with both hands as his stomach roiled. The whiskey had burned all the way down and showed no signs of letting up. Buckner hoped the maid had remembered to empty the chamber pot, and then remembered there wasn't any maid.

But luckily, there is a window, he thought with a sly smile.

The hallway was unlighted and he bounced off both walls going down the narrow corridor fishing for his key. He managed to hum a few bars of a nameless tune as he fitted the key into the lock and opened the door. Buckner tossed off his hat, still reeling a bit from the effects of the booze, and stumbled toward the bed. Ambient lighting from the full moon shone in through the window, so he could make things out. He sank to his knees, feeling around under the bed for the chamber pot, but couldn't find it. Swearing, he grabbed the bed railing and stood, half pushed himself erect, and took a box of matches from his coat pocket as he moved to the dresser. Buckner opened the box, spilling most of the contents. Swearing, he blinked and felt around the top of the furniture before finally snaring one of the pesky little matches. His fingers gripped the glass of the lamp and he lifted it to light the wick. As he struck the match and watched the flame ignite, he caught a glimpse of something off to his right, but the window...

Buckner froze.

A large man stood in the shadows. Buckner could tell little more about him except that one of his hands held a huge gun, which, thankfully, was pointed at the floor.

"Don't light the lamp," the man said his voice low. There was something familiar about it, but Buckner couldn't figure out what it was. He didn't move until the match burned down, searing his fingers. Hastily shaking it out, he swallowed, suddenly felt almost sober.

"You armed?" the man asked.

Buckner shook his head.

"Turn around," the man said.

Buckner did as he was told.

The man moved forward and Buckner felt a strong hand tracing over his body. He felt a sudden urge to void his bladder, but didn't dare search again for the chamber pot. He hoped he wouldn't soil his pants.

Buckner looked back over his shoulder and saw the man step back into the shadows and holstered his gun.

"Who are you?" he asked.

Buckner swallowed, still feeling the urge to urinate.

"My name is Julian H. Buckner, the Third," he said in a voice fraught with trembling weakness. "Who're you?"

"Don't light the lamp."

"Never mind that. You don't look like no outlaw. What you doing here?"

"I'm a writer. Dime novels." He gestured toward the chair by the bed, which held his traveling bag. "I have some in there I could show you."

The man ignored the offer. "Who are you to McTavish?"

"No one. I hardly know the man."

"You seemed pretty cozy in the saloon."

It was like a veil being torn away from Buckner's eyes. This man was the Negro drifter who'd been in the saloon earlier. Buckner felt like an iron hand was gripping his bowels. "You're the..." He stopped himself, realizing he had to choose his words carefully. This man did, after all, have a gun. "You're the drifter from the saloon, aren't you?"

The man said nothing for a solid ten seconds, then spoke. "I'm Deputy Marshal Bass Reeves." He held open his vest and in the moonlit room Buckner could discern a silver star.

"What do you want from me?"

"I'll ask you again, what are you to McTavish?"

"Nothing." Buckner felt a renewed urgency to empty his bladder. "Look, he wants to be like Jessie James. The man's a self-absorbed maniac."

"Tell me somethin' I don't know."

Buckner swallowed again. "He wants me to write about his exploits in one of my novels. He thinks he's got this magnificent plan."

The man was silent for a few moments, then asked, "What's McTavish got planned?"

Buckner swallowed. Was this Negro really a marshal? He remembered the bloody lawman stars. Could this be some kind of a test of his loyalty?

"I don't know," he blurted out.

In the semi-darkness Buckner saw the man's hand reach for the butt of one of the twin pistols holstered around his waist.

"Mister," the man said, his voice low and even. "I ain't got the time nor the inclination to play. What's McTavish got planned?"

Buckner was on the verge of pissing his pants. He thought about asking if he could please use the chamber pot, but couldn't find the words to speak.

"I ain't got all night," Reeves said.

His voice held power and authority. Perhaps he really was a lawman, as he said.

"He's going to rob the train," Buckner blurted out. He watched to see if the man was going to draw his gun and shoot.

He didn't, and Buckner relaxed a bit.

"The train? When?"

"In the morning. Around first light." Buckner swallowed, recalling the plan that McTavish had so meticulously laid out for him. "The train's already coming from Denver with a load of gold bullion."

"How's he know when it's coming through here?"

Buckner let out a small laugh. "A couple of the soldiers told one of the girls in the saloon that they had to get up at three in the morning for a changing of the guard when the train pulled in. He's got look-outs posted. They'll fire off three shots when the train comes around the bend."

"How's he figure to stop a train? He gonna block the tracks?"

Buckner felt a flood of excitement now. He shook his head. "He's got it all worked out. There's a set of dead-end tracks that were supposed to lead to the town here, but they were never finished. There's a switching lever on the regular tracks that'll transfer the train into those dead-end ones. Once the engineer realizes it and hits the brakes, it'll be too late. McTavish has got three wagons and a bunch of horses ready to take the gold."

"There ain't no guards?"

"There's a contingent of soldiers on board guarding it. Twenty of them."

"Twenty soldiers? And McTavish thinks he can take all of them?"

"He's got…" Buckner stopped. Dare he say more? If McTavish found out it would be a certain and unpleasant death.

"He's got what?" the man asked.

Buckner breathed in and out several times. Certain death might be a possibility from McTavish, but he wasn't here now, and Buckner could sense Reeves was someone to be obeyed. "He's got a Gatling gun. A Bulldog. He's going to use it to kill them all. He's got two men to fire it to wipe out the soldiers and then he and the rest of his men will drive the wagons in and take the gold."

"A Bulldog? Where'd he get it?"

"I don't know. He said he took it from some soldiers."

"What time's this supposed to happen tomorrow?"

"The fort's about forty miles from here," Buckner said. "If it leaves there at four, like it's supposed to, it should be passing by the old Temptation station around six."

The black lawman said nothing for several seconds, and then moved to the open window. Buckner could discern a rope of some sort hanging outside. Reeves thrust one arm through the opening and grabbed the rope. He paused and turned.

"Best for you if'n' you forget I was ever here," he said.

With that, the rest of his body went through the opening and he disappeared into the night.

Buckner barely managed to find the chamber pot in time.

On the outskirts of Temptation City

Buckner slid off the back of the wagon as it came to a halt. It was early morning but still dark out. They were about half a mile from the town now, out where the set of dead-end tracks ran out. The place where the ambush was going to take place and a lot of men were going to die.

"Keep the horses and them wagons outta sight over by them trees. The rest of y'all git over in that gulch," McTavish yelled as the members of his gang dismounted and handed their horses to Crow. "Finn and Tomás, move the Bulldog into position. A couple of you others git over to the other side of them tracks in case any of them blue bellies jump out the other side of the car. We'll get 'em in a cross-fire."

Buckner watched as the outlaws spread out in the darkness, each man armed with a rifle and at least one handgun apiece. It was going to be bloody. It was going to be a damn turkey shoot. The soldiers wouldn't have a chance, unless…perhaps that Negro lawman had managed to warn them. But how could he? It had been less than five hours since their late-night conversation. Hardly time enough to ride all the way to the fort to try to intercept the train. Still, Buckner hoped he had tried. At least that way there was chance that the carnage that was certain to unfold once the train derailed would not occur.

He heard the distant crack of three gun shots; the signal from the lookouts that the train had veered onto the dead-end tracks. It would be here in less than a minute.

Buckner caught a glimpse of McTavish's leering grin as he watched the big half-breed and the unctuous Mexican roll the Gatling gun up the embankment and aim its barrel toward the tracks. Buckner heard a distant chugging sound and could imagine the wispy trail of blackish smoke filtering upward from the engine's chimney as the train approached. As the sound grew louder he began to feel a slight vibration under his feet and the train veered suddenly to the right, coming in their direction.

McTavish laughed and turned to Buckner.

"Better git by them horses, Julia," he said. "Yer 'bout to see some real shooting and a helluva lot more killin' than you ever seen before."

Reeves and Bear crept through the darkness as the dawn began to edge up behind them. They'd tied their horses in a small clearing and traversed the rest of the way on foot. Reeves knew that he had to let part of the plan play out. There was no way he could stop the approaching train. He saw men moving about fifty yards ahead and dropped to a prone position motioning for Bear to do the same. The ground vibrated with the weighted momentum of the approaching train. Reeves could barely discern it in the nascent light. Down by the tracks, three of McTavish's men scampered across the other side and crouched down.

"We gonna have to take that Gatlin' gun first," Reeves said.

"Then what?"

Reeves pointed. The black, massive shape of the train engine became visible, barreling toward the end of the tracks and the inevitable crash. It chugged along, not slowing at all, and then suddenly bucked and jumped as the front end ran out of rail. The momentum carried the huge, metal beast forward, but it veered left along a slight declivity in the ground, the rest of the cars jumping and twisting like a gigantic sidewinder slithering through a field of grass. Twisting metal screamed in the darkness, accompanied by the sound of artificial thunder.

"We gotta move now," Reeves said, getting to his feet. "We take out the Bulldog, then you move to the other side of the train and take them three over there."

"What you gonna be doin'?"

"Takin' care of the rest of 'em."

He began a quick trot toward the outlaws. The train finally jerked to a stop after traveling about twenty or thirty feet. The cars shook with a residual tremble.

Several of the outlaws began a series of cat calls. The side door of the boxcar opened and three soldiers jumped out, trying to hold their rifles at the ready. The soldiers continued to pour out the open door, but many staggered and fell. The roar of the first burst of the Bulldog tore through the still dark surroundings to more cheers and yelling. The rounds hit the side of the boxcar, missing the soldiers.

"Turn that damn thing a little to the left, dammit," someone shouted from the embankment. Reeves recognized the voice: McTavish.

Reeves was almost there now. He saw the big half-breed lifting the end of the Gatling gun, rotating it to aim the barrel toward the emerging troops. The Mexican who'd roped Bear held the crank.

"That one's mine," Bear said.

Reeves covered the final yards in ten steps and slammed into the big half-breed. The big man grunted and fell to the side, the derby hat flying off his head. The Mexican whirled and pulled out his gun, but Bear kicked it out of the Mexican's hand.

The big breed pushed himself off the wheel of the Bulldog and grabbed Reeves' arm. Reeves punched the big man's face. The breed grunted and spit out blood. Reeves hit the man again, this time flattening his nose. The breed was quick for a man of great size and lurched forward, encircling Reeves in a bear-hug. Reeves felt the enormity of the breed's strength, and wondered if it was greater than his own. He exhaled and tried to take another breath, but could barely fill his lungs. The giant exerted more pressure and Reeves thought his ribs would break. He pulled his arm from the encircling grip, swung his elbow into the breed's jaw and then repeated the elbow blow to the man's temple. The pressure eased for a second and Reeves got both of his hands under the breed's chin. Pushing back with all his strength, Reeves felt the pressure easing more. He bent the giant's head back and felt the big arms weakening. Reeves chopped a blow into the other man's throat and the breed's grip broke. The giant staggered back, a savage expression on his face. He reached downward, his hand coming up with a gun, but Reeves already had his out, the hammer cocked back. Reeves squeezed the trigger and the flash from the barrel burst over the breed's face. The giant dropped like a felled buffalo.

Reeves turned to see Bear and the Mexican engaged in a knife fight. Before Reeves could point his revolver at the outlaw, Bear parried a thrust and shoved his own knife deep into the Mexican's gut.

"Who's *mierdra* now?" Bear asked in a guttural voice.

A gunshot sounded as a round bounced off the wheel of the Bulldog. Reeves holstered his gun and grabbed the Gatling gun, lifting it to swivel the barrel toward the group of outlaws. He grabbed the handle and rotated the crank. The circle of barrels rotated, sending out flames half a foot long, and the badmen fell screaming in a twisted heap. Bear moved off to the side with his Winchester and said, "I'll get them other three."

Another bullet whizzed by Reeves and he rotated the crank again.

Three more of the badmen jerked and fell.

Reeves saw three figures about thirty feet away running up toward the buckboard that had housed the Bulldog. He took what cover he could behind the gun and drew his Peacemaker. Before he could fire he saw the three men scrambling onto the buckboard. In the increasing daylight, Reeves saw the three were Crow, McTavish, and the dime novel writer. McTavish held the dude in front of him and fired his gun over the other man's shoulder.

The bullet pinged off the Bulldog's barrel. Reeves ducked and came up, aiming at the departing buckboard, but he couldn't get a clear shot. The writer was still in the way.

Reeves turned and glanced at the scene. There was little movement among the remaining outlaws, all of whom lay scattered in twisted, unnatural positions.

Bear was suddenly beside him now.

"Got all three of them."

"Get our horses," Reeves said. He holstered his weapon and looked toward the soldiers who were positioned in a haphazard manner outside the boxcar. Most of them still staggered drunkenly in circles.

That crash must've knocked the hell out of them, Reeves thought.

"I'm Deputy Marshal Bass Reeves. Who's in charge of you men?"

A couple of the young troopers looked around. A young looking man in a uniform with a pair of yellow bars on his shoulders stepped up.

"I am," he said. "Lieutenant Cates."

The lieutenant looked like he still had a set of whiskers a cat could lick off.

"Indian!" one of the young soldiers yelled and pointed his rifle at Bear, who was walking up with two horses in tow.

Reeves jumped forward and grabbed the barrel, lifting it upward so that it fired harmlessly into the sky. Bear turned and held the reins of the frightened animals, keeping them from rearing up.

"Hold your fire, you damn fool," Reeves said. "Him and me just got through savin' your sorry asses."

The young trooper sheepishly looked at the ground. "Sorry."

"You best be, boy," Reeves said, glaring at the man as he released the rifle barrel.

"Only good Injun's a dead Injun, huh?" Bear said with a smirk and a wink.

"Nobody fire unless I give the order," the young lieutenant shouted. He turned to Reeves. "Marshal, what do you need us to do?"

Reeves glanced around. "Take custody of those outlaws, or what's left of them. And commandeer them horses. You should probably send a couple of men back to the fort to tell 'em what happened."

The lieutenant nodded and gave the sergeant the orders.

"Tell 'em to be on guard," Reeves said. "There may be some bushwackers between here and there."

"Right," the lieutenant said, and relayed that order as well.

Reeves stepped over to his horse, grabbed the saddle, and swung up onto the animal. Bear did the same.

"You gonna need another engine out here to right this mess," Reeves said, gesturing at the tangle of metal of the derailed cars.

"Wait," the lieutenant said. "Where are you going, Marshal?"

Reeves reined his horse in the direction of Temptation.

"McTavish and Crow ran off in that buckboard," he said. "I got a score to settle with them."

"But, they've got a head start. How will you catch them?"

"It's what I do," Reeves said as his boots kicked into the gray horse's flanks and the animal shot forward. "If'n any of them outlaws is still alive, I'll be back to collect 'em."

Temptation City

Reeves saw the abandoned buckboard in front of the saloon. The tracks had been easy to follow. He'd figured as much. McTavish most likely wanted to stop and grab whatever stash he had before hightailing it. Reeves swung his leg over the saddle and signaled for Bear to dismount as well. He took out one of his Peacemakers and said, "They must be in the saloon. Watch out for the bartender. Got a scattergun behind the bar."

"He's mine," Bear said, patting his Winchester.

They approached the batwing doors in rapid fashion, stopping on either side of the opening.

"McTavish," Reeves called out. "This is Deputy Marshal Bass Reeves. I'm placing you under arrest for the murder of them six Deputy Marshals."

A loud laugh sounded from within, and McTavish yelled, "Come on in and get me, boy."

Reeves and Bear exchanged glances and burst through the doors, spreading out to each side as they entered.

McTavish leaned against the bar, a bottle of whiskey and a glass in front of him, a wry smile on his face. Crow stood off to the bearded man's right, grinning, and the bartender held a shotgun on top of the bar. Buckner, the dime novelist, sat off in the corner looking terrified.

"Yeah, I had a funny feeling 'bout you the other day, boy," McTavish said, bringing the glass of amber liquid to his lips. He drank, exhaled with seeming satisfaction, and slammed the glass onto the bar. "How'd you find out about them Marshals?"

"You left one alive," Reeves said. "He told me who bushwacked 'em before he died."

McTavish snorted a laugh. "Careless of me."

"I'm taking you back to Fort Smith to stand trial for murder," Reeves said. He was holding his Colt down by his leg. His thumb cocked back the hammer, having a feeling how this one was going to play out. "You gonna come in peaceably?"

McTavish licked his lips and he shook his head. "Not likely." With that, the bearded man whirled, drawing out his pistol and firing it.

Reeves dodged to his left, figuring the bullet would veer to his right. He brought up the Colt Peacemaker and squeezed the trigger. McTavish grabbed his substantial gut and leaned back against the bar. Reeves switched his aim to Crow, who was now pointing a gun as well. Both weapons exploded simultaneously and Crow's damaged head exploded like a ripe melon. Bear's Winchester roared and the bartender dropped the shotgun and twisted, grabbing at the rows of glasses and bottles next to him. The glass shattered as it fell to the floor a few seconds before he did.

McTavish struggled to raise his gun again, and Reeves shot the man between the eyes. The outlaw's head jerked back, then forward, and he fell forward onto the wooden floor, a crimson puddle widening around his slack, bearded face. Reeves moved forward and checked each man, then stooped and snatched the gun from McTavish's limp fingers. He tucked it into the side of his gunbelt and kicked the outlaw over. Reeves leaned down and ripped the Deputy Marshal's star from the gunman's shirt.

"You ain't deservin' to wear this," Reeves said. He pocketed the star and then went behind the bar to retrieve the metal rod with the five other stars strung on it.

"I come for these," Reeves said, holding up the circle of stars, "and for my gun, too."

He looked over at Buckner, whose eyes were as wide open as a pair of white dinner plates.

"Marshal," the dime novelist said. "I can't believe it. You stopped all of them."

Reeves said nothing. He walked over to the writer and stood in front of him. "You got something to write with?"

Buckner nodded and took out his pencil and notebook.

"Need you to put something down for me," Reeves said. "Nice and neat." He recited the mailing address that dying Frank Moore had given him.

Buckner printed it clearly on the paper and handed it over.

Reeves stared at the written words, admiring the clean, angular lines, but not able to decipher them. He carefully folded the paper, put it in his pocket, then took out his last silver dollar.

"Here you go, Mr. Buckner," Reeves said, flipping the dollar to the writer.

Buckner caught the coin and looked at it. "Marshal, you don't have to…"

Reeves held up his hand and shook his head. "I give them to folks that helps me. And helps the law."

He reached into his pocket and removed the star that the dying Marshal had given him. His strong hands gripped the iron bar and he pulled the ends apart, opening the circle, and then slipped the sixth star onto the bar with the others.

"Got to return these," Reeves said. He turned toward the door.

"Ready?" Bear asked.

"Yeah," Reeves said, looking around. "I reckon our job's done here."

He strode toward the doors and went out.

"Wait," Buckner running after him. "I'd like to do a story about you."

"Not interested," Reeves said.

"But…"

"No buts," Reeves said, already in the saddle. "I can't read noway."

Buckner's jaw hung slack.

Reeves turned to Bear. "Let's get a move on. It's a long way back to Fort Smith."

"But, wait," the dime novelist said, pushing through the doors and onto the street. "I didn't even get a chance to talk to you, to thank you, to… what's your name, again?"

Reeves turned in his saddle and glanced back at the dime novelist. "Bass Reeves. Deputy Marshal."

He turned forward and urged his horse to a trot, never looking back.

THE END

The Legend of Bass Reeves

I read the first volume of Bass Reeves stories, and thought it was fantastic. When Ron Fortier told me that he planned a second volume, I jumped at the chance to be part of it. Let me first say that I am honored to be in such a distinguished company of fellow writers as Milton Davis, Derrick Ferguson, and especially my buddy, Mel Odom. I also feel honored to be able to pay homage to Deputy Marshal, Bass Reeves. He was a man who overcame incredible odds to serve and protect and uphold the law. Having spent most of my adult life in law enforcement, I felt a special kinship with this remarkable man. I hope my story does him justice.

I first heard of Bass Reeves when I read a book called *Bill O'Reilly's Legends and Lies*, by David Fisher. It devoted one chapter to the Black marshal who started out as a slave and became a highly effective lawman. I immediately sought more information about him. Reeves was described as a big, powerful man who was a crack shot and held a high regard for justice. He was appointed a Deputy Marshal by Judge Isaac Parker in 1879. Parker was called the "Hanging Judge," and had a fearsome reputation for administering stiff and often lethal sentences, but also a high regard for the law. He instilled this sense of justice into Reeves, who, by all accounts was a very honorable man. Although he couldn't read or write, Reeves had a remarkable memory. He would commit the names of those wanted on the warrants and brought in many of the dangerous outlaws alive to stand trial. Reeves' primary area of operation was the Indian Territories, which was regarded as a very dangerous and lawless place. The territory included what later became the state of Oklahoma, but at the time was divided between five Native American tribes, the Choctaws, the Chickasaws, the Creeks, and the Cherokees. The tribes had their own law enforcement agency, called the Lighthorse, which was a mounted police force. The Lighthorse had no jurisdiction over white men, however, and the territories quickly became a magnet for outlaws and riffraff fleeing justice. To say the least, the region was a very dangerous place.

Reeves could speak several Native American dialects, and often asked one of the Lighthorse to accompany him on his quests. In writing this story I also wanted to pay homage to the great westerns that thrilled me in my youth. I couldn't resist including a few references to some of my favorite western books and movies *The Comancheros*, *Badman* (aka, *The War Wagon*), and *Rio Conchos*. Astute western fans will be able to pick out those homages. I've always wanted to write a western as a tribute to a distant relative of mine, Zane Grey, so I'm grateful for this opportunity. And lastly, I'm extremely grateful to have been able to include an homage to a great friend of mine, David Walks-as-Bear. Bear, as I called him, was an American Indian (the designation he preferred over the current, politically correct "Native American.") He spent his life serving his country both in the military and in law enforcement, and I was honored to call him my friend. He was a very talented writer, and an expert on all aspects of American Indian culture. He was also one of the smartest guys I ever met. We lost him a few years ago, way too soon, and being able to bring him back for this story was like a gift from the Great Spirit he used to talk about.

I tried to stay true to the historical facts, while still imbuing a bit of the western mythology that I grew up watching and reading about. I also couldn't resist including the first machine gun and predecessor to the M134 Minigun that our troops use today, the 1877 Bulldog Gatling Gun. I've seen an actual replica of the Bulldog up close and personal, and had the privilege of turning the crank numerous times at the SHOT Show in Las Vegas. I also did a copious amount of research on the handguns and rifles of the era.

I did my best to pay homage to Bass Reeves, a great lawman, and to get everything pretty close to the way it really might have been back in the day. But if any astute readers do find a few anachronisms, I fall back on the standard defense of my dime novelist character, Julian H. Buckner, the Third, and put it off to artistic license.

MICHAEL A. BLACK - is the author of twenty books and over one-hundred short stories and articles. His latest novel is *Chimes at Midnight* and he is also writing the Mack Bolan Executioner series (*Sleeping Dragons, Deadly Salvage, Payback*).

THE BIXBEE BREAKOUT

By Derrick Ferguson

Once upon a time during the fall of 1894...

The prisoner wagon was a huge, cumbersome contraption that lumbered along like a buffalo with severe constipation. It creaked and wheezed and rattled, making enough noise to conceivably be heard for miles. But it was strong and escape proof and that was all that mattered. Three of the four men chained up inside had long ago given up their cursing and complaining. The driver of the wagon and the man riding alongside it didn't listen and didn't care anyway.

Said driver of the wagon pulled his buffalo hide coat tighter around his skinny body. He always complained of being cold no matter how hot it was. But then again, Tom Lucky complained about everything. A full blooded Chickasaw he was. He'd been one of the most respected, feared and honored members of the Chickasaw Lighthorse until one day he just up and quit without giving a reason why. He spent most of his days now drinking corn liquor and arguing with his three wives. But when Bass Reeves called him to cook and wrangle the wagon, he came.

Bass Reeves rode next to and slightly ahead of the wagon astride his huge white stallion, Cisco. He rode with his Winchester out, the butt resting comfortably on his right thigh, finger off the trigger. His eyes never stayed for long on one thing, but constantly roved the terrain. They were traveling through open rolling grasslands and being in such open country while being pursued made Bass nervous.

"How far behind us you figger they are?" Tom Lucky asked suddenly. Bass hated when he did that. If he wasn't mumbling to himself in Chickasaw, Tom engaged in periods of silence that lasted hours and then

142

would all of a sudden start talking as if he'd been holding a conversation with you all that time.

"Don't have any good idea. That's why I got Sonny watching our back door. However far behind they are it won't take them long to catch up to us with this wagon moving as slow as it does."

Indeed. Not only was the wagon not built for speed by any stretch of the imagination, it was pulled along by mules. Animals noted for their stamina, endurance and strength. Not their speed.

"Dammit, Bass…you got any notion a'where the hell we is at?"

"Still a good two days out from Fort Smith. There's a town somewheres around here. Bixbee, as I recall."

"Yeah, I know Bixbee. Haven't been there in damn near twenty year, though."

"What were you doing in Bixbee?"

"I wasn't law then. Huntin' bounties. Tracked down a couple of bad actors scalped a fambly of Mexicans over yonder by Coyote Point."

Bass nodded. Hearing hoof beats off in the distance he turned in the saddle, bringing the Winchester around. Tom already had his hands on the sawed-off double barreled shotgun he kept on the seat next to him at all times. "It them?"

"Naw. It's Sonny."

Sonny Calvera rode up to join them. An able, capable posseman, he'd worked with Bass four times now and as a result was quickly making himself a name for himself in the Indian Territory as a posseman to be relied on. As a result it was getting harder for Bass to engage his services as other Deputy Marshals were quick to hire him when he was available.

"How far behind us are they?" Bass asked, handing Sonny his canteen. Sonny took a swig of water, swished it around in his mouth, spat it out. Having rinsed the trail dust out, he then took a decent drink before answering.

"I'd say we got three, mebbe four hours on 'em. They ain't pushing their animals as hard as I did mine." Sonny patted the neck of his sweating, trembling horse whose legs were visibly wobbling. "They know we can't go but so fast with this rig." He nodded at the wagon.

"There's a town not far from here. Bixbee. We can hole up there. I'll speak to the Sheriff. Maybe he and his deputies can give us a hand holding onto our prisoners. I can get a wire to Judge Parker and ask him to send for reinforcements." Bass sighed. "Best way to handle this is to fort up in the jail. Soon as we hit town, get all the food and water we'll need for three, mebbe four days and just hold the jail."

A sardonic voice came from the wagon. "Or you could just do the smart thing and let me go, Bass! I'll make a deal with you. Right here and right now. You let me out and I'll wait here for my pa. You do that and you got my word I'll call it even. We'll go on our way and you won't ever see me again."

Bass rode over to the wagon. Three of the prisoners didn't even bother looking up. It was the fourth one doing the talking. A lean, hatchet-faced young man whose baby blue eyes would have been adorable if they weren't the eyes of a lunatic. This was the one Bass Reeves spoke directly to. "You're a rapist, thief and all-round murderin' no-good, Slade Pritchard. And I aim to take you back to Fort Smith so that Judge Parker can give you a fair and lawful trial before he hangs you. So you fix your mind around that and keep your mouth shut before I shut it for you."

Slade Pritchard grinned crazily but held his tongue.

Bass turned Cisco around and returned to Sonny and Tom who asked; "You know this Sheriff in Bixbee, Bass?"

"Nah. Never met him. I knew the old Sheriff, man name of Miller. Killed by his sister-in-law a two, threes years ago, I heard. This new man was appointed by the town to take over." Bass looked over at Sonny's horse. "You sure your animal's gonna make it?"

Sonny again patted his steed on the neck. "Provided we don't have too much further to go. How far is it to this Bixbee?"

"Maybe three miles. No more than five."

Bixbee came into sight as Bass and his party crested the slight rise of a hill. Bass heard Sonny sigh with relief. He tried not to show it but he was worried about his horse. Bass sympathized. He was powerful fond of Cisco himself having raised him from a colt. They rode on into the town, ignoring the openly curious looks of the townspeople. Bass flipped back the lapel of his ankle-length duster so that the Deputy Marshall badge pinned to his double breasted Baker City vest could plainly be seen. Along with his midnight black suit and bolero hat with the extra wide brim that kept the sun out of his eyes and astride the powerful white stallion, Bass Reeves made an imposing figure indeed.

Bass was pleased to see that the combination Sheriff's office and jail was constructed out of stone. The roof was not made of wood but of slate. He nodded to himself in satisfaction. If he and his men were forced to fort up in here they wouldn't have to worry about being burned out. He motioned for Tom and Sonny to take the wagon around to the back of the jail. He himself went to the front. He climbed down off Cisco, tied him to the hitching rail and went on in the Sheriff's office.

Sitting behind the desk placed catty-corner in the far side of the office, a sandy-haired man still on the light side of thirty looked up from his paperwork. He took in Bass with eyes that were alert, wary and guarded but not afraid. "Afternoon, mister. Can I help you with something?"

Bass walked over to the desk, taking out an envelope from the inside of his vest. "I'm Deputy U.S. Marshall Bass Reeves, out from Fort Smith. Here are my credentials, signed by Judge Parker himself."

"No need for that. I don't reckon there isn't a lawman in the territory that hasn't heard of Bass Reeves. I'm Sheriff Larry Durham." He stood up to shake hands with Bass. "Pleasure to meet you, Marshall. What brings you to Bixbee?"

"How many jail cells you got?"

"Four."

"You got any prisoners in 'em?"

"Just ol' Jerome. He gets liquored up and gets rowdy once in a while. I throw him in a cell until he sobers up."

"That's all?"

"That's all. You want to tell me what all this is about?"

"I got four prisoners I'd like to put in your cells for a couple of days at most."

Durham shrugged. "Sure. Don't see why not."

"Wait until you hear the whole story first. One of 'em's Slade Pritchard."

Durham whistled long and low before saying; "How'd you hogtie that crazy bastard?"

Bass grinned. "Wish I could take full credit for it. Truth of the matter is that I wasn't even lookin' for him. I was pickin' up one of my other prisoners in Slowbank. Word was sent to me by a saloon gal name of Millie Suggs who worked in Edlerdale, 'bout ten miles north of Slowbank. Said that if I wanted Slade Pritchard, he was coming to see her and she'd get him good and drunk so I could take him with no problem."

"You weren't worried it could have been a trap?"

"Seems that Millie Suggs had a cousin who also worked the saloons. Pritchard paid this cousin for her favors but didn't think he got his money's worth. Beat the cousin so bad she was pissin' blood for a week. Millie's been courting Pritchard ever since then, figuring she'd get him drunk and cut his throat her ownself. But then she got to thinkin' how Slade and his pa bragged on themselves about how they've never seen the inside of a jail and never would. She got to thinking that a better revenge would be to have him sittin' in a jail cell, waiting to get his neck stretched."

Durham nodded. "Let a woman put her mind to getting even with you then you best to go ahead and drown yourself. Where you got your bad men at?"

"Told my men to bring the wagon 'round to the back of your jail."

Durham nodded and led the way. They went through a stout, thick wooden door and through the holding cell area. Two cells on either side. Durham unlocked the back door, opened it. Tom Lucky still sat in his usual spot. Sonny climbed off his horse and stood to the side of the door.

Bass made the introductions. "That's Tom Lucky up there holding the shotgun and this here's Sonny Calvera. Tom, Sonny, this is Sheriff Durham. He's agreed to let us put our prisoners in his jail for a spell. Tom, you stay up there until we get them in."

Tom nodded, rested the barrels of the sawed off shotgun on his bony right knee. He tossed down a large iron ring of keys to Bass who walked to the rear of the wagon. "Okay, boys—here's how it's going to go. Felton, Harmon and Roberts—you three climb down first. Slow and easy. We'll lock you up first. Sheriff Durham, I'd be obliged if you'd assist me with that. Sonny, you stay here and keep your rifle on Pritchard at all times. He raises his ass up from the floor of that wagon, you send him to hell for dinner."

Slade Pritchard cackled as if Bass had just told the funniest joke he'd heard all that day.

The transfer of the three prisoners went without incident. They weren't real badmen. Felton was supposed to stand trial for disturbing the peace. He'd shot the windows out of a saloon in Fort Smith. Judge Parker had let him go with the understanding that Felton was supposed to return a week later to be tried. But terrified of Judge Parker's reputation, Felton lit out. Damn fool. Judge Parker would at most have given him the option of paying a fine or ten days in jail. But for running out, Judge Parker was obliged to make an example out of him now. He'd probably do six to eight months hard labor.

Harmon had shot a man named Washburn he claimed was keeping company with his wife. Washburn asserted that since he was not blind he could see quite clearly that Harmon's wife had a face that greatly resembled the south end of a northbound mule. As such he had no desire to keep any sort of company with Mrs. Harmon for any reason at all. Harmon laid for Washburn and shot at him, hitting him in the right calf, so bad was his aim. But brother Washburn had been so terrified he'd fainted right on the spot and so Harmon went on the run, his impression being that he'd killed the poor sot.

Roberts was a simple thief. He robbed a hardware store of $14.

Most would think it waste of time for Bass to go after these three when there were so many true desperadoes, murderers and outlaws still roaming the territory unhanged. But that wasn't the way Judge Isaac Charles Parker looked at it. To him a lawbreaker was a lawbreaker and he expected his Deputy Marshals to pursue a misdemeanant with the same vigorous zeal with which they pursued a felon. "Let no guilty man escape!" That was his battle cry, the words he lived by and woe betide the Deputy Marshall who did not live and breathe those words with the same fervor as Judge Isaac Charles Parker.

Felton, Harmon and Roberts climbed out, the chains on their ankles and wrists clanking as they did so. Bass and Durham marched them into the jail where Bass unlocked their manacles and motioned that they should all get into the same cell. The three went in meekly and looked mournful as Bass slammed the jail cell shut. Durham unclipped his keys from his belt and locked the door.

The noise roused Jerome, sleeping in another cell. He sat up on his bunk, yawned and scratched the stubble on his cheek. "Mornin, Larry. What all's goin' on here?"

"You never mind, Jerome. I'll be letting you out directly, providing you're sober."

"Sober enough, I reckon." Jerome looked at Bass with open amazement. "Who's that?"

"Like I said, never you mind."

Bass and Durham went back out to the wagon. Bass pointed his Winchester at Pritchard. "Before you come on out I need you to believe me when I say that the first time you move any way I don't like, I'll kill you. We in agreement on this?"

Pritchard cackled again. "Don't you worry, Bass! I aim to be alive and well to watch my pa skin you alive! I'm gonna enjoy watchin' that! Wouldn't miss it for the world!"

"Come on out, then. Slow and easy."

Pritchard did as he was told, all the time grinning wickedly at Bass as if they were going out for a night on the town. Bass and Sonny kept their Winchesters trained on Pritchard until he was in a cell by himself. Bass gestured that Durham should shut and lock the door. Durham frowned slightly. "Aren't you going to take the shackles off?"

"His shackles stay on. Close and lock the door."

"You took the shackles off the others."

"They ain't Slade Pritchard. Close and lock the door."

Durham shrugged and did as he was bid. Pritchard did a little jig, jingling his chains. "I kinda like the sound they make, don't you?"

Bass said to Sonny. "You see to your horse then come on back. Tell Tom to get the wagon hid somewhere, tend to the mules and get right back here."

Hearing the jingling of Durham's keys, Bass turned around. Durham unlocked the door to the cell Jerome occupied and motioned for him to come on out. "Go on, Jerome. Go on home. And try to stay sober for at least three or four days straight, okay?"

Jerome came on out, looking in Pritchard's cell with something like horror at the outlaw, still doing his madcap jig. "You really Slade Pritchard?"

"You bet your ass, bucko!"

Jerome now swung his gaze at Bass as his expression changed to open astonishment. He spied the badge and said, "You really a Marshall?"

"Deputy Marshall. Bass Reeves is the name. And I do believe Sheriff Durham done told you to git."

And Jerome did git, scurrying out of the holding cell area and out the front door as fast as his two feet could carry him.

Bass and Durham returned to the office. Durham gestured at the cast iron potbelly stove in a corner. "Help yourself to coffee if you want, Marshall. My deputy Jack Farrell makes a mean pot."

"Do believe I will. Then I'll thank you to point me in the direction of your telegraph office so that I can send off a message to Judge Parker."

Durham took off his hat and flopped in his chair. "No telegraph office. Best I can do is send one of my deputies to Fort Smith to inform Judge Parker of your situation."

"How many deputies you got?"

"Three. All solid, capable men."

"You send one, that still leaves us with six guns to handle Pritchard's gang. Good." Bass poured himself a cup of steaming hot coffee black as midnight.

Durham frowned. "Gang? What gang?"

"Slade Pritchard's pa Boone is wearing out horse flesh tracking us. I 'spect he'll be here in three, four hours. My plan was to fort up here in your jail until help arrives. You send your man now and he pushes it with a good horse, he can be in Fort Smith in a day and a half. Then it'll be another two days for a posse to get back here. We can hold out that long, I reckon."

Durham's frown increased. "Now hold on there. You didn't say nothing about a gang coming to bust Slade out. How many guns you figure Boone Pritchard got with him?"

"Don't rightly know. My man Sonny was tracking him. We'll ask him when he gets back."

"The Pritchard gang isn't to be taken lightly, Marshall. There's a reason why they haven't been put down by now."

"They're men who put on their pants one laig at a time. Same as you and me, Sheriff. You pump a bullet in them, they fall down. Don't build them up in your mind to be more than what they are. They ain't nothin' but a lawless band of no-count owlhoots, is all."

Once he was let out of jail, Jerome went directly to The Old Alehouse, his favorite saloon. It was the favorite saloon of most of the town's citizenry and Jerome knew enough people there that he could always successfully bum drinks. He strode through the batwing doors and headed straight for the bar neither looking left or right. He threw coins down on the rough surface of the bar and said; "Gimme a double, King. And keep 'em coming."

The bartender looked at the money with some mild surprise as he poured the double. "Paying with your own money for a change. It ain't Christmas and it ain't your birthday. What's the occasion?"

Jerome tossed back the double shot of whiskey as if it were water and indicated that King should pour him another. "I just seen something I ain't never thought I'd see in my life and if that don't call for me getting drunk, I dunno what does."

"What happened? Saw your wife naked?"

Jerome tossed back the second double shot and waved his hand for a third. "I just saw me a nigger with a badge throwing four white men in our jail. And one'a them white men is Slade Pritchard."

Jerome spoke loud enough to be heard by those standing or sitting near

"I just seen something I ain't never thought I'd see in my life

him and conversation ceased. Some of the men looked at each other in confusion as if they couldn't possibly have heard what they thought they heard.

The bartender frowned at Jerome. "You must be drunk already. I think I'm gonna have to cut you off, Jerome. I don't appreciate you coming in here tellin' crazy stories. Somebody might take you serious."

"Dammit, I ain't drunk! I just spent two days in the jail sleepin' off the last one. I was laying in a cell when Larry Durham comes in with this big black buck dressed as good as any white man. Got a big ol' Deputy Marshall badge pinned to the fancy vest he's sportin.' And he had four white men he put in the jail cells and slammed the door on 'em. One'a them he put in a cell by himself and didn't that son of a bitch start doing a jig like a drunken Irishman while he still had his laig and arm chains on. Larry Durham said the nigger Marshall should take those chains off and the Marshal said he wasn't takin' no chains off'n Slade Pritchard and that was that. So help me God, that's the truth."

A murmur of amazed conversation went around the saloon. Marcus Murray stood up. A big-bellied man with graying hair he still moved with the lightness of a younger man despite the obvious lines of age in his face. "Waitaminnit. Let me get this straight. A Negro Deputy Marshall you say? How long this been going on?"

"Mister, how long you been in the Territory?" somebody inquired.

"Me? Just got out here a couple weeks ago. I'm a newspaper man from back east. I write for The Chronicle. Heard there were a lot of wild stories out here. Sounds like I just found one. How long you been letting Negro marshals lock up white folks?"

"Mister, you stay out here in the Territory long enough you'll see stranger than that."

This got a loud and long round of laughter and some applause from the assemblage of day drinkers. But Murray wasn't amused.

"I got nothing against Negro marshals but certainly they're only supposed to lock up Negroes and Indians, ain't they? They can't go around locking up white men anytime they please."

Another man spoke up. "Jerome, this black marshal. He a real big man, 'bout six feet? He got a big ol' bushy mustache? Trim real neat an' tight? Wears two Colts? Wears 'em so that the butts are turned inward?"

Jerome nodded enthusiastically. "That's him! You describe him better'n than I could have! You know him?"

The man nodded. "Seen him in Fort Smith a couple of times. That's

Bass Reeves. He's a Deputy Marshal, all right. Damn good one from the stories I heard about him."

Murray frowned. "That's all well and good but what gives him the authority to go around arresting white men?"

"Judge Parker, that's who. And out here, Judge Parker is God because God Hisself didn't want to be bothered looking after The Indian Territory. So he left it to Judge Parker to take care of it. And he do a helluva job."

"I take it this Judge Parker is a white man?"

"White and Christian."

"And he gives a Negro the authority to arrest white men?"

"Ol' Bass arrests anybody Judge Parker gives him paper to arrest. White, black, Indian, European or Asian. It don't make no never mind to ol' Bass. There are those who hearin' that Bass has paper on them elect to leave The Territory and save themselves from a hangin' or a bullet. Bass Reeves is bad medicine any day of the week and that's a fact."

"Well I will be well and truly damned." Marcus Murray hooked his thumbs in his braided leather suspenders. "I knew this was a savage and untamed wilderness but this beats all hollow. This is the sort of thing my readers back home would love to read about. Think I'll amble on over to the sheriff's office and lay me an eyeball on this here Bass Reeves for myself."

Deputy Anton Baines laid his badge on the desk in front of Sheriff Durham. "Sorry, Larry. I like working for you but I didn't sign on to take on a dozen guns. And that's how many I heard was in the Pritchard gang."

Bass spoke up from where he stood next to one of the windows. He was inspecting the thick wooden shutters with the cross shaped gun ports in the center. "If we all fort up in here we can hold the jail. They can't burn us out and there will be more than enough of us to keep watch front and back so that they can't take us by surprise."

"I don't work for you and I ain't talking to you," Baines snapped at Bass over his right shoulder. He turned back to Durham. "You heard what happened over to Yellow Rock 'bout five months ago? Sheriff there arrested one of the Pritchard gang. Terry Walker, I believe. Well, the gang couldn't burn down the jail but that didn't give them no pause at all. They started burning down the town. When the Sheriff finally did let

Walker out, the Pritchard gang killed the sheriff and his deputies anyway. Five or six other folks were dead, four buildings burned to the ground. I don't mind goin' up against regular thieves and bandits but the Pritchard gang…" Baines trailed off. He turned back to Bass and said, "Look, I don't mean no disrespect, Marshal. I heard a'you and I know you're supposed to be good an' all…but I got a wife and three kids."

Bass nodded and said, "Look, how 'bout this, can you ride to Fort Smith and tell Judge Parker the spot we're in and ask him to send help? It's only a two days ride."

Baines visibly brightened up. "Sure! Sure! I can do that! All I got to do is let my missus know I'm gonna be gone a spell."

Durham spoke up. "Go on over to Fred Lowry's and borrow that palomino of his. That's the fastest horse I've ever seen in my life. Explain to him the situation and if he gives you any guff remind him that I took his side when he had that dispute with Jim Grandee last summer."

Baines nodded. "I sure will do that, Larry. You can count on me. I'll be on the road inside of an hour." Baines paused on his way out the door long enough to stick out his hand. "Again, I meant no disrespect, Marshal. But you got to see how it is."

Bass shook his hand and merely nodded. Once the door closed behind Baines, he looked at Durham. "Guess you really only have two solid, capable men, Sheriff."

"Don't go taking that tone, Marshal. Baines is all right. This is the first time he's bailed on me."

"You got a wife, Sheriff? Chirren?"

"I got married two years ago. We're expecting our first child this November."

"And you're here."

Durham shrugged. "Baines ain't me."

"I got a wife and family, too. And the day I use them as an excuse for not doing the job I swore an oath to do is the day I take off this badge for good."

The door opened again and a slight, rawboned young man wearing a deputy's badge bustled into the office. He spied Bass and his eyes goggled in surprise. "Son of a bitch! It's true! You is Bass Reeves!"

Durham said; "This here's Jack Farrell, Marshal. It's his coffee you've been enjoying. How'd you know Marshal Reeves was in town, Jack?"

"Jerome, of course. Once you let him go he went straight to The Old Alehouse and started telling about how there was a nigger with a badge… "Jack caught himself and looked at Bass with sheepish embarrassment.

"Sorry, Marshal. Just repeating what Jerome said."

"It ain't like I ain't heard it before, son. Go on with your story."

"Jerome went to telling everybody how Bass threw four white men in jail. And that one'a them white men was Slade Pritchard. Well, there's some writer fella from back east who said he was gonna hunt up Dave Sweeney and come on over here to make sure ev'rythin' was on the legal up and up."

"Who is this writer fella and who's Dave Sweeney?" Bass wanted to know.

"The writer's a fella named Murray. Been out here 'bout two weeks. Says he's lookin' to write some stories to send back to his newspaper. Dave Sweeney is our local lawyer. He's okay."

"I ain't got time for no nonsense, Sheriff. We got to start getting ready." Bass looked hard at Jack. "Best you know right up front what you're getting' yourself into, boy. It's true that I got me Slade Pritchard back there. His daddy and their gang are on their way here. I aim to fort up in this jail until I can get help from Judge Parker."

"Baines is going to go ride for help, Jack," Durham added.

"So that's why he was runnin' down the street like his ass was on fire," Jack chuckled.

"You in or you out?" Bass demanded.

Jack adjusted his gun belt with both hands. "I ain't ever run from a fight. And I ain't ever let Sheriff Durham down. I'm in. What do you need me to do?"

"Lay your hands on all the food and water you can and bring it back here. Once we lock up, ain't none of us leaving."

"I'm on my way."

"You seen Hymie?" Durham asked. Hymie Price was his third deputy.

Jack shook his head. "Not for a couple of hours. Can't imagine he hasn't heard what's going on. He should be checkin' in most anytime now."

"Okay. You see him you tell him he's to come see me straightaway. And you go tell Jerome to take his big mouth home else I'm gonna throw him in the same cell with Slade Pritchard."

As Jack went out, Sonny and Tom came in. Bass grunted, "I was just about getting' ready to go lookin' for you two. What took you so long?"

Tom answered; "We went to the livery stable. The proprietor refused us service. Said that he couldn't take the chance that the Pritchard gang would find out he was helpin' the law and burn him out. Sonny and I had to scout around to find someplace safe to leave the rig and his horse. We found an abandoned storehouse on the west side of town. Then we had to scrounge up feed and water for the animals." Tom chuckled. "Sonny convinced the livery owner to feed and water the animals down at the storehouse. He's quite the convincer, our Sonny is."

Bass sighed. "Okay, here's how it lays so far. Sheriff Durham was good enough to send one of his deputies to Fort Smith. The other two will stay and help us out. Along with the sheriff here that gives us three extra guns and three extra pairs of eyes. That means nobody can sneak up on us. But I want you to stay back there with Slade, Tom. You keep that shotgun right on him at all times, no matter what you hear goin' on out here. You understand me?"

"I sure do."

"And if you hear me sing out, you kill him. You understand me?"

"I sure do."

"Best get you some sleep while you can. You can eat later."

Durham pointed. "Go on through that door, old timer. There's a cot in there you can stretch out on, grab you forty winks."

Tom nodded. "Much obliged, Sheriff Larry."

"What do you want me to do, Bass?" Sonny asked.

"Scout the town. Be back here in an hour. Go out the back way."

Sonny nodded and departed. Durham frowned. "Anything you want to know about Bixbee I can tell you, Marshall. I've lived here five years now."

"In an hour Sonny Calvera will know his way around this town better than you."

"He's that good, huh?"

"Yep. He's that good."

Hearing a knock at the door, both Durham and Bass turned and said, "Come on in!" Bass chuckled and said; "Sorry 'bout that, Sheriff. Habit."

The door opened, immediately filling with the bulk of Marcus Murray who stood there for a few seconds, taking in both Bass and Durham. "You'd be Sheriff Durham?" He came on in the office, sticking out his hand to shake Durham's. He then whirled around, again holding out his hand. "And you'd be Deputy Marshall Bass Reeves, then. I trust you have some sort of identification or credentials asserting to that?"

"You haven't said who you are, yet." Bass replied.

"I beg your pardon. My name is Marcus Murray. I'm a journalist. I write for The Chronicle, one of New York's finest newspapers." Murray held out a business card. "I assure you that my name and my writing are well known."

Bass merely glanced at the card, tucked it away in a vest pocket. "What's your business here, mister?"

"I'm waiting on Mr. Sweeney, a local lawyer and when he arrives I would then like to see your warrants to arrest those four men you have in Sheriff Durham's jail. If you have no such warrant then we shall compel you to turn these prisoners over to Sheriff Durham until such time it can be determined if you do have the legal right to arrest these men."

Bass actually laughed. A rich, chocolatey laugh full of warmth that came from his belly. "Mr. Murray I honestly don't know whether I should buy you a drink or beat your ass. I truly don't."

"This is no laughing matter, sir, I can assure you!"

Sheriff Durham stood up, leaning on his desk with his knuckles as he said, "Mr. Murray, Deputy Marshal Reeves is well known to me and many in the territory as being one of Judge Parker's most trusted lawmen. I don't understand exactly what it is that you want here."

"I find it incredible that a Negro lawman is empowered to arrest white men. I find it even more incredible that other white men are apparently quite comfortable with him doing so. Now, if Mr. Reeves arrests other Negroes and Indians, that's all well and good. But for him to go around arresting white men...well, how do you know he's arresting the right white men? Those four men he's got in there could be innocent men he's wrongly apprehended because he couldn't find the right men he was after. How do you know?"

"I don't make a habit of arresting the wrong men, Mr. Murray. I wouldn't be working now if I did."

"I thought you folks back east were pretty open-minded about Negroes," Durham said. "That's how I always heard it."

"Our attitudes are very progressive in the east, Sheriff. But still, there are some lines that shouldn't be crossed." Murray smiled at Bass. "I assure you that there's nothing personal about any of this, Mr. Reeves."

"That's Deputy Marshal Reeves. You call me anything except that and I'll knock all them nice shiny teeth right outta your head."

Murray gulped. "There's no need to.."

"You are interferin' with a Deputy Marshal in the lawful performance of his duties. You don't get gone in the next thirty seconds I'll arrest you and throw you in the cell right next to Slade Pritchard."

Murray whirled around to Durham. "You're just going to stand there and not do anything? Say anything?"

"Just this: I'll hold the cell door open for Deputy Marshal Reeves while he's putting you in there."

Murray fumed. "I'll have some very interesting stories to write for my paper, I assure you."

"And I think that's all you're doin' here, Mr. Murray," Bass said. "I think you're just tryin' to kick up some dust so you'll have some exciting stuff to write about for that fancy newspaper you work for. You stick around until the Pritchard gang gets here and you won't have to worry. Things will be pretty damn excitin' around here and that's gospel. Now git before I get mad."

Murray started for the door but was blocked by Dave Sweeney coming in. "And where have you been?" Murray raged. "I needed you here five minutes ago!"

"Just been talking with some folks," Sweeney said. He walked over to Durham's desk. "Larry, the talk's all over town that the Pritchard gang is coming to bust Slade Pritchard out. Is it true?"

Durham sighed. "Yeah, yeah, it's true. Deputy Marshal Reeves here asked if he could use my jail to hold him. He's got Pritchard back there with three other prisoners."

Dave Sweeney looked profoundly unhappy. "You oughta know better than that. Once you heard Reeves had Slade Pritchard you should have told him to push on. Boone Pritchard ain't gonna stand for his son being taken to Fort Smith to hang."

Bass cut in. "He could catch a bullet right here, counselor."

Sweeney rounded on Bass. "See here, Reeves, I know your reputation. But you also have a duty to protect and safeguard the lives of innocent civilians. If the Pritchard gang comes to Bixbee there a chance somebody's going to get killed."

"Nothin' wrong with folks getting kilt," Bass replied. "Of course, if it's the right folks doing the killing kills those that need killing. But I ain't aiming on killing' nobody less'n I'm pushed into doing so. And now I want the both of you out of here. An' spread the word that from this moment on, any man comes within ten feet of this here jail is going to catch a bullet."

Sweeney turned back to Durham. "Whose jail is this, Larry? Yours or his?"

Now Durham was beginning to look as mad as Bass. "You got no call to be throwing that in my face, Dave. Marshal Reeves and I are both lawmen. I'm obliged to help him out just as he would be obliged to help me if the shoe were on the other foot.

"Your obligation is to the people of this community that voted you into this office, Sheriff!" Murray said, stepping forward to stand next to

Sweeney. "Reeves brought this unwanted trouble to your town-ARK!"

Murray was cut off in mid-sentence by Bass grasping him by the back of his neck with his left hand while his right lifted up his suit jacket and laid hold of the waistband of his belt. Bass swung Murray around as if he weighed no more than a kitten. He hustled Murray over to the door of the office. "Open it," he said in a voice that plainly indicated he meant what he said. Bass threw Murray out of the Sheriff's office, propelling him on his way with a lusty kick to Murray's posterior. The newspaperman went flying into the street, kicking up a cloud of dust as he landed.

Bass brushed his hands together. "Told you that you call me anything other than Deputy Marshal, I'd knock your teeth out. You're getting off easy. This time." Bass turned to Sweeney. "You wanna leave the same way he did?"

Sweeney went out the door, throwing at Durham over his shoulder; "This isn't over, Larry. Not by a damn sight."

Bass closed the door. "I figured that the lawyer should be on your side, Sheriff."

Durham sighed heavily. "I apologize for Dave Sweeney. Ever since I took this job he's been shoulder-to-shoulder with me. We work together fine. You got to understand that these people ain't used to situations like this, Marshal. The most that ever happens in Bixbee is a couple of fights on Friday and Saturday night down to the saloon. We haven't had a shooting here for six months. Nothing happens here. Now we got a notorious outlaw locked up in our jail and his gang is coming to break them out." Durham sighed again, picked up his hat and put it on his head. "Now, as to that newspaper fella, I don't know what to tell you. I ain't talked to him much. I said a couple of words to him when he first come to town. But I do that with everybody new. Nothing special there. He seemed to be a harmless enough fella."

"You ever deal with any newspapermen before Murray?"

"Me? Naw. We don't have no newspaper here in Bixbee. Only time I read a newspaper is when I go to a town of some real size and importance like Fort Smith. You?"

"Ran into a writer fella 'bout ten years ago or so. Like this Murray he was lookin' for stories to write up and fell in with a bad bunch ramrodded by a real bad actor name'a McTavish. The writer fella helped me out, though. He wasn't a bad sort."

"What was his name?"

Bass had to think for a minute. It had been a while ago and he'd only met the writer twice. That first time in Temptation City and then a few

"Reeves brought this unwanted trouble to your town-ARK!"

years after that in Fort Smith when the writer had come to meet up with Judge Parker. "Buckner. That's it. It was some long-winded fancy name he had but Buckner was his last name."

"I think I recall hearing something about that. Wasn't this McTavish lookin' to rob an Army train carryin' gold?"

"That's the rascal. He wanted this Buckner to write up stories 'bout him. Make him famous."

"I'm surprised he didn't write up any stories about you."

Bass shrugged and left it at that. In fact, Buckner had written up a bunch of dime novels about Bass even though Bass had told him not to. But Buckner was a fair man. He'd sent Bass a check and copies of the dime novels he'd written about him. Even though Bass couldn't read his wife Nellie could and she had read the dime novels to Bass to pass the time during long winter nights after their children had gone to bed. The dime novels were silly and frivolous but they did make Bass and Nellie laugh and she was both proud and pleased that her husband's name was known back East, so Bass never made an issue of it.

Durham put his hat on and headed for the door. "I'm going to go on out, see if I can gentle folks down, put a stop to some'a the wilder rumors. I might be able to talk some'a the men into helping us. If we can get even three or four men with rifles up on the roof that'll help."

Bass nodded. "Agreed. I'll stay here with my prisoners."

"You do that."

Durham left and Bass locked the door behind him. Slade Pritchard cackled from the holding cell area; "Sounds like you got yourself a whole mess'a problems, there, Bass!" Even though the door was closed, there was a small hatch at eye level that the Sheriff and his deputies could hear if a prisoner was in distress. Bass mumbled a curse under his breath. He should have made sure that hatch was closed so that Pritchard couldn't hear their plans. But who knew that Murray and Sweeney would come busting in talking such craziness?

Bass walked on back there to find Pritchard sitting cross-legged on the floor of his cell. He grinned up at Bass. "I'm thinkin' that maybe you should be rethinkin' your options, Bass. Don't you?"

"I don't see why I should. I got you and I'm keeping you. It's just that simple."

"My daddy's got a dozen men with him. You got what, three? Four? You can do figures. And yours don't add up. But I'm a right generous guy so I'm willin' to forget all'a this if'n you let me go right now, give me a horse and let me ride on out."

"And how am I supposed to explain how you got away?"

"That ain't my problem. That's yours. But at least you'll be alive to explain it. You go the way you're goin' now and you're gonna get a lot of folks killed along with yourself."

"I think I'll just play this out and see how far I can go. Okay by you?"

Pritchard shrugged and stretched out on the floor of the cell. He placed his hat over his face. "Suit yourself, Bass. You be sure and wake me up when my daddy gets here, won't you?"

Larry Durham figured that most everybody with a voice and an opinion would be over to the Alehouse and he was right. He could hear the noise of shouted argument before he'd gotten halfway there. He pushed in through the batwing doors to see that most of the men in town were in there. Spying Durham coming in, Marcus Murray bawled; "Well, well, well! Here's your brave sheriff now, folks! The same sheriff who stood by and did nothing while Reeves laid his hands on me and kicked me out what is supposed to be his office as if I were no more than a common ruffian!"

"You had it coming, Mr. Murray. You take an awful lot on yourself." That was all Durham could get out before he was surrounded by men all yelling excited questions at him. At least until a balding, short man with a lean build pushed them back, clearing a space around Durham.

"Now just hold it, hold it! The Sheriff can't speak if'n you're all screaming at him!" Paul Ross glared at the men he shoved back until they settled down then he turned around to face Durham. "Okay, Sheriff. Exactly what's goin' on?"

Durham outlined the situation, filling in the blanks for those who hadn't been in the Alehouse when Jerome had first babbled what he knew. He finished up with; "Reeves has got Pritchard in our jail and he's asked for my help. As an officer of the law, I'm obligated to render him any and all assistance."

"No, you ain't!" Clint Perrell pushed his way forward. A crotchety sort was he. He also was the town's banker and as such was not only Bixbee's wealthiest citizen; he was the most influential as well. "You were appointed by me and the other leading town citizens to be Sheriff! That means you work for us! And we're giving you an order to tell Reeves to take that cutthroat and get him out of town before his gang gets here! If he's not in

Bixbee they won't have any reason to stay and murder the lot of us."

"I can't do that, Clint."

"Can't or won't?" Murray demanded. "This town is your jurisdiction. If you tell Reeves to move on, he's got to move on. Since this is your jurisdiction, you're the one in charge, not him."

"That's right!" Perrell agreed. "I don't care who Bass Reeves is or who he works for. He still doesn't have the authority to come into a town that has a sheriff duly appointed by the citizens of that town and tell us what to do. Now you march yourself right on back to that jail and you tell Reeves to light out right quick!"

Durham frowned severely. "I thought you folks took your law seriously here in Bixbee. First time you get a chance to help out a Deputy Marshall and you want to turn your back. Seems to me we could be gainin' ourselves a lot of good will from Judge Parker if we helped one of his men out. Having Judge Parker owing us a favor is worth more than money in the bank if'n you ask me."

"I don't give a rat's ass for Judge Parker!" Perrell roared. "He's sittin' in his office over to Fort Smith protected by his Marshals and the United States Army an' here I be with just you and three deputies between this town and the Pritchard gang! Now you get yourself on over to that jail and you tell Bass Reeves he's to take Slade Pritchard outta Bixbee right now! And if he refuses to do it then you turn Slade loose!"

"I can't do that. He's not my prisoner."

"Lemme put it to you this way, Larry." Paul Ross stepped forward. "Either you can do what we say or we can come down there ourselves and turn Pritchard loose. You bein' the law here we'd rather you do it. But if it comes down to us doin' it then so be it. But it's going to get done."

Durham glared at the assembled faces around him. Grim faces full of determination. "It ain't law turning a wanted man loose. A man who's a known thief and murderer. We let him go he'll go on to murder more innocent people. Steal their money. Rape women and orphan children. You can live with that?"

"Larry, we got our own families to look out for," Ross replied. "Yeah, Pritchard will go on to do just that. But it don't do nobody no good for some of us to get killed and he gets turned loose anyway. You can see that, can't you?"

"What about Bass Reeves? He ain't never lost a prisoner yet. Don't you have any confidence in him?"

"I don't know Bass Reeves!" Perrell howled. "But I do know what the Pritchard gang is capable of! Now you go do as you're told, dammit! You tell Reeves he's got thirty minutes to turn Pritchard loose or we're coming down there to turn him loose ourselves!"

Bass opened the door for Sonny Calvera. He walked in, wearily sat down in the nearest chair, pushing his shoulder-length straight black hair out of his face. "How you holdin' up, Bass?"

"I'm okay. How 'bout you?"

"I could do with a couple hours sleep. I canvassed the town. I can draw you a map if you like."

"Do that. Then find somewhere to grab yourself some sleep."

Sonny nodded, propped his rifle up against the chair he'd been sitting in then went over to Durham's desk. He pulled open drawers, looking for some paper he could draw a map on. He ran across a stack of old wanted posters in the bottom drawer and grunted in satisfaction. The top drawer contained some pencils. He sat in Durham's chair and began drawing his map. As he did so he said, "You think this Sheriff is gonna stand with us when the Pritchard gang comes?"

Bass stood by one of the windows, keeping an eye on the street. "I think so. He's a good man. One of his deputies has said he'll throw in with us. The one you saw go out when you came in? That's him. The one that rode for help I'm sure he'll do it 'cause he sure as hell didn't want to be here. There's a third deputy but I haven't seen him."

"You figger he's run off?" Sonny's hand moved rapidly as he continued drawing.

"Sure he did. By now everybody in town knows what's going on. That other deputy came right here to report in when he heard. But not that third one. He went and found himself a hidey-hole and he's gonna stay there until it's all over. Just as well. If he ain't gonna help I'd just as soon not have him here getting in the way."

Sonny stood up. "Here you go." He walked over and handed Bass the map. "Here's where we are. I figger they ain't gonna sneak into town. Not that's there's a whole lot of ways to sneak into Bixbee. Anyway, they'll want to make a big show, scare the townsfolk and scare us too, for that matter."

"Okay. Go on and get yourself some sleep. We're just gonna wait here for them."

"And then what?"

"I'll figure something out."

"Could be the odds are too high against us this time out."

"The trick is to lower the odds."

"Yeah? And how do we do that?"

"Like I said; I'll figure something out. Go on and get some sleep." Bass could see Larry Durham coming back to the office and from the way he walked Bass reckoned that things hadn't gone very well talking to the good citizens of Bixbee.

Durham came in, took off his hat and flopped into his chair. "They're powerful mad, Bass."

"How mad."

"They say if'n you don't turn Pritchard loose, they're comin' over here to turn him loose themselves."

"Is that so?" Bass laid his Winchester down on Durham's desk. "You mind if I go and talk to them?"

"It won't do any good. Their minds are made up. You go over there and all you'll do is make them madder."

"Then it won't do any harm, will it?" Bass headed out the door. "I'll be back in ten minutes."

Durham got up from his chair and closed the door behind Bass. He looked out the window. Bass strode toward the Alehouse as if he were keeping a rendezvous with Doomsday, his duster flapping around his legs, swinging his arms purposefully. Durham looked over at Sonny. He'd placed two chairs together as a makeshift bed and stretched out on them to catch a nap. "What does he think he's going to do?"

Sonny yawned before answering. "He's going to explain a few things, is all. Don't worry about it. Bass is a real good explainer."

Bass walked up the steps, pushed open the batwing doors and went into the Alehouse. Durham didn't know what to expect. He just stood there, watching with narrowed eyes as he tried to figure out what could possibly be going on over there.

After about two or three minutes, men started leaving the Alehouse. Most of them were walking real fast while a few trotted along and three or four were actually running. In about five minutes flat, the Alehouse cleared out. Bass Reeves stepped outside and surveyed the empty street. He walked back to the Sheriff's office, spurs jingling in the silence.

He came on back in the office, picked up his Winchester and resumed his place at the window.

Durham gawped in amazement. "What….what did you say to them?"

Bass looked over at Durham. "I just explained the situation is all."

"Wha…that's all you did? Just explain?"

Bass broke out into a big, toothy smile. "I'm a real good explainer, Sheriff Durham. Real good."

From where he sat, Sonny Calvera chuckled softly and slid down further in the chair.

"Bass."

Bass Reeves turned over on the cot. Once Tom Lucky had gotten his sleep, Bass took the cot to get his. He felt as if he'd just closed his eyes but a glance at the clock on the wall across from Durham's desk told him he'd been asleep for just about an hour. Durham himself stood in the doorway. Bass had insisted the door be left open. Bass sat up, dry washing his face. He stood up. "What's the problem?"

Durham replied in a voice grim and gray; "They're here."

Sonny Calvera had taken up a position at one of the windows. Tom Lucky was in back with his shotgun pointed right at Slade Pritchard. Jack Farrell was at the locked back door, also with a shotgun just in case the Pritchard gang decided to rush it or attempt to burn through.

Bass looked out the window, Durham at his side. A dozen men on horseback in the middle of the street, facing the sheriff's office. The man in the middle spoke, raising his voice to be heard clearly; "Is Bass Reeves in there?"

"I'm Deputy Marshall Reeves."

"I 'speck you know who I am."

"I do indeed. You'd be Boone Pritchard."

"My understanding is that you've got my boy locked up in that there jail."

"I do."

"I'd take it as a personal favor if'n you'd see your way to turn him loose. And then we'll ride on our way with no gunfire having been exchanged and no loss of life."

"That's not going to happen, Boone. Best you and your men ride on and consider Slade a lost case. All'a you got paper on you but I'll settle for what I got. I'm not a greedy man."

Boone Pritchard took off his hat, wiped his sweaty forehead and sighed heavily. A big, barrel-chested man, he looked like he should be riding a bigger horse. The one he currently rode was barely big enough to qualify as a pony. "I heard you were both a smart man and a reasonable one."

"I like to think I am."

"You're not bein' one of either right now."

"Boone, there ain't much point in you and I spendin' a lot of time on this. I done told you I ain't lettin' Slade go. Now, it's up to you what you want to do. I give you a suggestion. You don't want to take it, that's up to you."

"My guess is that you got a man with a gun pointed at my boy."

"Double-barreled sawed-off shotgun in fact. I give the word, my man pulls the trigger."

"You ain't looking at this from my point of view, Bass. This ain't personal. But the Pritchards got a reputation for not going to jail or being hung. Now, I let you take Slade back to Fort Smith, Judge Parker is gonna hang him for sure."

"I can practically guarantee it."

"Then you see my problem."

"Nobody told you to raise your boy up to be a murderin' no good so-and-so like you, Boone. You bring him up to follow in your footsteps I guess he takes the consequences that come with the family trade."

"Now you're bein' insulting."

"Nope. Just honest."

Boone Pritchard sighed again and replaced his hat on his head. "Okay. I guess we'll have to do this the hard way then. You must have heard what I done at Yellow Rock."

"Some."

"Well, I'm gonna do the same thing here. Me an' the boys are gonna go on over to that saloon there and have us a couple of drinks. And if by a reasonable amount of time Slade isn't walkin' in there to have a drink with us we're gonna commence to burning down this town, one building at a time. Now, what do you say to that?"

"I got a box of matches you can borrow."

Boone Pritchard actually laughed behind that one. "You're a piece of work, Bass Reeves. I give you that. But I 'spect once you smell the flesh of the good people of Bixbee cookin' you'll be changing your mind. Be seeing you soon." Boone Pritchard turned to his left side and made with hand signals. One man broke away from the group and rode over to the alley. He got off his horse, tied it to the nearest hitching post and then took up a position where he could see the back door. From where he was, he could easily keep anybody pinned down that attempted to sneak out. Boone Pritchard and the rest of his men directed their horses toward the Alehouse, riding slowly. And why should they hurry? They had all the cards.

Durham turned to face Bass. "You better know right here, right now that I got no intention of lettin' Pritchard burn down this town. I'll turn Slade loose my own damn self. I got a responsibility to the people of this town and if that means I got to turn your prisoner loose to ensure their safety then that's what I'll do."

Bass sized up Durham with calm eyes. "You didn't say that before, Sheriff."

"We had options before. Now we don't. The Pritchard gang is here and they mean what they say. Unless you come up with another option, I'm turning Slade loose in five minutes."

"I do have another option. One that will most likely get us all killed."

"Let's hear it anyway."

Bass said to Sonny, "Go get Tom and Deputy Farrell and bring 'em here. I only got time to lay out this plan one time."

Sonny Calvera eased open the roof hatch. Inside, Bass and Durham put out all the lights so that illumination would not be seen from the street and thereby warn the Pritchard man watching the rear door of the Sheriff's office. Sonny had divested himself of his coat, his belt, his spurs, any article of clothing that might catch or make noise. This part of the plan had to be carried out in absolute silence in order to pull off the rest. Sonny softly closed the hatch. He blessed the noise coming from the street. The clip-clop of horse hooves on the hard-packed earth mingled with the rattling of the occasional wagon or buggy as folks hurried on home. Twilight signaled that night was coming on swiftly. The noise helped but Sonny knew outlaws. They depended on their ears just as much if not more than their eyes. Same as him. Sonny's ears and nose had saved his life more times than he could count as he had heard or smelled something odd before he saw it.

On his belly, he crabbed his way across the roof. Bass said he would give Sonny two minutes to get in position and not a second more. Sonny made it to the edge of the roof and waited. It wasn't more than maybe twenty seconds before he heard the rear door of the office open slowly and cautiously. The Pritchard man at the end of the ally spied the door opening. Now was the crucial part. Would he take the bait and move in closer or would he simply fire off a warning shot and raise a hullabaloo, bringing the rest of the gang? Sonny knew what he would do. Simply stay where he was and shoot anybody coming out. But this man wasn't Sonny.

Sure enough, he crept closer, his gun in hand, the barrel gleaming slightly in the dying day's light. Sonny threw himself over the edge of the roof and landed right on the Pritchard man, slamming him to the ground with such force that the sound of cracking ribs could plainly be heard. His gun went flying from his hand. Before he could make a sound, Sonny had his Russell butcher knife thrust into the man's neck. Blood spurted and the Pritchard man died without making a sound.

Bass Reeves threw wide the rear door and Jack Farrell ran outside, seized the dead man by his clothing and hauled him inside the jailhouse. The whole thing had been accomplished with no noise to speak of. Slade Pritchard and the other prisoners observed all this in silence. All of them were securely tied up and firmly gagged so that they could not raise a hue and cry that might give warning. Bass turned to the waiting Tom Lucky. "You're up. You sure you can get inside?"

Tom grunted. "Who's gonna pay attention to an old Chickasaw?" Tom secreted his sawed-off under his buffalo hide coat. "An' if they do I can stall 'em long enough for Sonny and Jack to get in position."

Bass nodded, gestured to Sonny and Farrell. "Get goin' you two. You got ten minutes then me and the Sheriff are comin' in."

Sonny took a few minutes to strap on his gun belt and shrug into his coat. Farrell silently handed him his Winchester. The two men exited the building and trotted into the alley. They took a minute to make sure that they were clear then quickly turned the corner and sprinted down the street. At the same time, Tom walked briskly across the street, heading for the Alehouse.

Leaving the dead body where it was, Bass returned to the office. Durham waited there, watching the Alehouse. "Your man's almost there, Bass."

Bass nodded. He took his Colt Single Action Army Revolvers out of their holsters, laid the left one on the Sheriff's desk while inspecting the right one.

"You weren't kidding' when you said that this plan of yourn could get us all killed. However way you count it up it's still eleven guns to five."

Bass nodded as his twirled that revolver back into its holster with his right hand while picking up its brother with his left. As he inspected that weapon he said; "True. But I'm countin' on a couple of things. One, the element of surprise on two levels. They won't expect us to be walkin' through the front door bold as brass to take them on. Two, they won't be expectin' Tom, Sonny and your man Jack. My experience with a gang of outlaws is that once you cut down two or three of 'em, the rest tend to give up. Most outlaws much rather do the killing than the dyin'."

Durham said nothing. Wiped his mouth with the back of his hand. "Your man's inside. Reckon we should start on in?"

"We gotta give him, Sonny and Jack time to get in position. You sure you ready to go through with this?"

Durham picked up his Winchester. "No. But let's go on and get 'er done."

Tom Lucky pushed open the batwing doors of the Alehouse and stumbled on inside. No longer was his stride sure and confident. Now he adopted the halting, shuffling gait of an old drunk. He allowed his face to go slack and half-closed his eyes. In the past this had proved enough to get him by. In his experience most white men were dumb enough to think all Indians were drunk all the time anyway.

Although it seemed as if Tom didn't look around him, he carefully noted where the Pritchard gang members were. They were occupying three tables they'd more or less shoved together over to the right side of the saloon and were busy imbibing as much liquor as they could toss down their gullets. Tom noticed three or four men he took to be locals way down at the far end of the bar, drinking quietly and talking even more quietly among themselves. Most of the usual patrons of the Alehouse had run off when Bass Reeves had come in earlier. And those who had come back in had left once the Pritchard gang arrived. The ones at the end of the bar were those whose craving for alcohol outweighed their common sense. Tom hoped they would have the brains to dive for cover once the shooting started. There wasn't going to be time to pick out who was who.

The bartender stopped his serving to bark at Tom, "What you want in here, chief?"

In answer, Tom mimed throwing back a shot of liquor.

The bartender frowned but he was not one to turn away business just because of the color of a man's skin. "You got money? Real money, American money. I don't wanna see none'a that wampum."

In silent answer, Tom pulled his left hand out of the pocket of his buffalo hide coat and opened it, showed two silver dollars lying in his palm. The bartender nodded and waved for him to come on over to the bar. "I'll give you drinks as long as your coin holds out. But when I tell you enough is enough you go on home to your squaw, savvy?"

Tom nodded and shuffled over the bar, threw a silver dollar on the sticky surface and watched as the bartender poured him a shot. The right hand pocket of his coat had a slit cut into it so that he could reach the handle of his sawed-off which rested in a special loop sewn into the inside of the coat. When the time came, Tom could simply lift up the fearsome weapon, flip his coat to the side and start blasting away. With his left hand he lifted the shot glass and tossed back his drink. With his right he careful and quietly cocked back the hammers.

The Pritchard gang had only given him the most cursory of inspections. They were laughing and carrying on with the easy carelessness of men who knew they were in control. Tom indicated that the bartender should give him another drink. This would be the one he'd make last. It wouldn't be long now.

Sonny Calvera watched Jack Farrell's back as he eased open the rear door of the Alehouse. "King don't ever keep this locked. Lotta men need to sneak out the back when their wives come in the front lookin' for them."

Sonny nodded and indicated that he should lead the way. They walked slowly and cautiously through the storeroom where cases of liquor and beer were stacked. Sonny noticed a couple of spare revolvers and rifles placed on top of a stack of crates where they could be gotten to easily. Sonny and Farrell helped themselves to the spare revolvers. They already had rifles and merely placed the extras out of the way where they could not be gotten to. Farrell gestured at a door. Sonny opened it into another hallway. From a half open door a third of the way down the hall he heard the sounds of rowdy conversation, full of laughter and profanity. "That leads into the Alehouse," Farrell whispered. He pointed to the other end of

"I'll give you drinks as long as your coin holds out."

the hall. "There's the staircase leads up to the second floor balcony. That's what we want."

The two men made their way down the hall. They moved quietly but thanks to the noise that the Pritchard gang was making, whatever creaking the floorboards underneath their booted feet made went unnoticed. Bass had rightly judged that Boone Pritchard's overconfidence would be the greatest asset to the lawmen. Pritchard relied on his fearsome reputation and what he had done to Yellow Rock to give him enough leverage in his favor. He would never dream that the fight would be taken to him and his gang.

Sonny and Farrell crept up the semi-dark staircase, staying to the sides of the staircase and not the middle. The stairs were more likely to make noise if they walked in the middle and while so far, nobody had heard them, this was not the time to get cocky or overconfident. All it would take was one wrong misstep and the whole plan could conceivably be shot to hell.

The two law men gained the landing and Farrell pointed with the barrel of his rifle at the door. "Go through there and we'll be on the second floor landing."

Sonny nodded. "Okay. We'll wait for Bass and the Sheriff. Soon as the shooting starts, we show ourselves. Okay?"

Farrell's eyes glittered with excitement as he nodded silently. He gripped his Winchester tighter and dropped into a crouch.

Bass Reeves and Larry Durham started across the street, marching side-by-side, shoulder to shoulder. Durham held his rifle cradled in his arms like a baby, his face stern and resolute. He was getting ready to go up against one of the most feared outlaw gangs in these parts. And he was doing it with one of the most feared lawmen in these parts. Pride shoved fear aside and bade it go hide in the corner until business was done. Bass had his revolvers and that was enough. If he couldn't get the job done with twelve shots then he had no business packing a badge. "You wanna do the talkin', Sheriff? This is your town, your jurisdiction."

Durham shook his head. "This is your play, Bass. You can talk for the both of us."

They stopped in front of the Alehouse. Bass looked at Durham. Durham looked back and nodded.

Both men walked up the steps, pushed open the batwing doors and entered the Alehouse. They just stood there as the raucous, rowdy conversation died away. One by one, the members of the Pritchard gang noticed the two lawmen standing there and they fell silent. Shot glasses hit the floor as they were dropped in surprise. Beer mugs were carefully placed down on tables.

Boone Pritchard burped loudly and finished off his beer before speaking. "When I said you were a piece a'work I didn't half know what the hell I was talkin' about, Bass. You either is the gutsiest son of a bitch on two legs or the stupidest."

Bass Reeves spoke in a voice that came from a realm of righteous justice: "Boone Pritchard, I am U.S. Deputy Marshall Bass Reeves and this is Sheriff Lawrence Durham. By the authority invested in me by the Honorable Judge Isaac Parker of the United States Court of the Western District of Arkansas we hereby place you and your associates under arrest for multiple counts of murder, mayhem and malfeasance perpetrated against the law abidin' citizens of this territory. I hereby direct you and said associates to divest yourself of all weapons and with your hands up willingly submit to summary and lawful arrest. Ignore this directive at your peril!"

Pritchard slowly stood up. "You know what your problem is, Bass? You take yourself too seriously. It's gonna get you kilt. Right here and right now."

"That your final word, Boone?"

"It is."

Bass drew his right hand revolver with a speed so blinding that he got off two shots that thundered in the sudden silence of the Alehouse. The outlaw on Pritchard's right went down with those two bullets in his chest, his gun still in the holster. Bass hadn't shot Pritchard on purpose. He wanted to take him alive if possible. And Pritchard was still fumbling with his own revolver. It looked as if Pritchard's fearsome reputation as a fast gun was his own fabrication.

The gang yelled, cursed. Some kicked the tables over and dived behind them. Others simply went for their guns, positive that they could cut down the two lawmen before they could get off any more shots.

Tom Lucky whipped his sawed-off, throwing aside his buffalo hide coat and squeezed the triggers. Three Pritchard outlaws went down under the devastatingly close blast from the fearsome weapon. They never even knew what hit them. One Pritchard man cursed and whirled around, banging away at Tom with more angry enthusiasm than skill. The wily Choctaw nimbly scrambled up on the bar, rolled over on it, scattering bottles and shot glasses. He fell behind the bar on his back. The bartender had dropped behind the bar when the shooting started. He glared at Tom. "Stinkin' red bastard!" he fumbled for his own shotgun he kept under the bar. Tom got out his revolver and shot the bartender in the face. It erupted in a red ruin.

Durham ran to the right, cocking and firing his Winchester as fast as he could. One Pritchard man took a bullet high up in his right shoulder and it whirled him around. As he did so, he reflexively pulled the trigger of his gun and shot one of his own compadres right in the left ear.

Bass stood his ground, drawing his other revolver and taking his time, placing his shots exactly where he wanted them. Two more Pritchard men went down.

Sonny Calvera and Jack Farrell emerged onto the second floor balcony and added their gunfire to what already sounded like a miniature war being waged inside the Alehouse. Sonny dropped two men before they even knew they were being fired on from above. Farrell got another one.

Boone screamed curses as he fired at Bass but so great was his rage that he wasn't even aiming. Still, the bullets whistled dangerously close to Bass. He could hear them go by. "Drop your gun, Boone! I ain't gonna tell you again!"

Boone replied with a highly inappropriate suggestion that Bass should indulge in sexual congress with his maternal parent. Bass shot him in the stomach for that. Boone shrieked and dropped to his knees, still firing at Bass. Bass shot him again in the stomach and Boone fell over, both hands clutching his ample belly. Crimson oozed out between his fingers and his curses mingled with the boom of gunfire.

Sonny yelped as a bullet whammed into his side and he fell over. Bullets whizzed around him, knocking quarter-sized chips out of the railing. He threw away his rifle, got out one of the stolen revolvers from the storeroom and stuck his hand through the railing, fired down at the outlaws. Farrell yelled like a Comanche as he also threw his empty rifle away and drew his guns.

Two of the Pritchard men took to their heels, legging it out the back door. Bass threw a couple of shots their way but he didn't pursue. He'd be content with what he had.

Seven of the Pritchard gang were down as well as Boone himself. Two of the men Tom Lucky had blasted with his shotgun were dead. The other one was still alive. He propped himself up against his dead compadres and blasted away at Durham, who'd taken cover behind the piano. It made a weird, warbling throbbing sound as the bullets went in and whanged around the piano wires.

Durham popped up from around the left side of the piano, took aim and put a slug right into the outlaw's forehead. He flopped over to join his partners in death.

The one that had been shot in the right shoulder stumbled to his feet, glaring at Bass through the thick haze of gunsmoke. He thumbed back the hammer of his gun, started to lift it.

"Don't do it, boy," Bass suggested.

"I'd rather die here than hang!" the owlhoot snarled. Bass nodded and obliged him. The impact of his two bullets slammed the gunman back into the bar. He slid to the already blood-soaked floor, coughing up a thick torrent of gore.

Bass walked over to where Boone lay, still holding his stomach. Bass slowly and calmly reloaded his revolvers. It could be that the two who had taken to their heels might regain some of what little courage they had and return to try and help their pards. But Bass didn't think so. Still, better safe than sorry.

"Goddamn your sorry soul to hell, Bass Reeves," Boone groaned. "You done kilt me. You kilt Boone Pritchard. I beg you to do me one favor. Don't let them stuff me and put me in a travelin' circus show like they done to Rome Scarborough."

"Hell no, Boone. I wouldn't let them do that. In fact, I'm gonna pay this town's doctor his weight in gold to keep you alive." Bass holstered his weapons. "I aim to take you in alive to Fort Smith for fair trial before Judge Parker before he hangs you. Right next to that sorry ass son of your'n. I figger it to be most fittin' that since the two of you robbed and murdered together you also hang together."

Bass Reeves watched as Tom Lucky supervised the loading of the roughly made coffins onto the top of the prisoner wagon. The inhabitants of the coffins would be buried in Fort Smith once they'd been properly identified.

"Your Judge Parker is going to be mighty pleased, Bass." Larry Durham came out of his office and stood next to Bass, thumbs hooked inside his gun belt, fingers slightly curled. "And your missus is gonna be happy as well. Lotta money up there on that wagon."

"I fully intend to see that you and your deputies get a share, Larry. You shared the risk. Only right that you share in the reward as well."

It had been three days since the shootout at The Alehouse. When Durham's deputy Baines returned to Bixbee with a posse of a dozen men deputized by Judge Parker to go assist Bass they found the situation under control. Boone Pritchard was still alive despite his best efforts to kill himself. Bixbee had two doctors, it turned out. The elderly Doctor James and his younger partner Doctor Gossett and both of them worked like heroes to keep Boone alive. They'd operated on him and got the bullets out, stopped the bleeding. Upon waking up after the surgery, Boone broke a drinking glass and attempted to cut open his own throat but was prevented by one of the doctors, routinely checking on the patient. Since the attempt, Boone had been tied down. Bass was determined to get him to Fort Smith alive.

A buckboard had been turned into a rolling bed for Boone and he lay in the back. Doctor Gossett had agreed to drive the buckboard to Fort Smith and tend to his patient. Bass assured him that Judge Parker would pay him handsomely for his trouble. Boone lay there, still tied up, glowering at Bass. To say that he was a poor loser would be putting it mildly indeed. Slade Pritchard sat inside the wagon but his look was that of a defeated man. Slade's eyes were no longer full of evil fun. They were the eyes of a man who knows that hell is waiting for him. The other prisoners sat quietly, trying their best not to call attention to themselves.

Now that Boone Pritchard's condition was stabilized, it was time to take the ride to Fort Smith. Sonny Calvera was also ready to ride. The gunshot wound he'd sustained during the shootout was more painful than anything else. He'd been shot up worse than that in the past.

"Matter of fact, why don't you ride on back to Fort Smith with us?" Bass said to Durham. "I can introduce you to Judge Parker and the two of you can sit down and have a nice long talk. Judge Parker can be a very generous man. Especially to those who assist his Deputy Marshals. If you take my meaning."

Durham grinned widely. "I do indeed. And I reckon Bixbee can manage without me. I sure don't have to worry about any owlhoots showing up to make trouble. Word's already fast spreading around about what happened here, I'll wager."

Bass nodded at Jack Farrell, approaching them from the right. "And you've got a good deputy to watch over things while you're gone. Whatever happened to that third deputy of yours?"

Durham shrugged. "Left town. I went over to his rooming house after things quieted down. The manager said Hymie Price came in, got his clothes and rode outta town like the devil was after him. Gave the manager his badge to give to me. Here comes that newspaper fella. Wonder what he wants?"

Marcus Murray stopped in front of the two men and gave them his widest, most amiable grin. "And there they are! The heroes of Bixbee!"

"Oh, so now I'm a hero, eh?" Bass replied.

"Any man that stands up to lawless outlaws is a hero in my book, sir! And more importantly, in my newspaper! I intend to file a story that will make Bixbee famous! And the two of you even more so. But as there is no telegraph here, I must prevail upon you to allow me to join you on the ride to Fort Smith."

Durham looked at Bass Reeves. "What do you say, Bass? That okay with you?"

Bass Reeves stroked his bushy mustached for a bit before answering. "Sure. Why not? I've always been the type to forgive and forget. Go get your stuff. We leave in an hour."

Durham looked at Bass with some surprise. "Didn't think you took to that fella, much."

"I don't. But Judge Parker might like to give him some stories he can write up for his paper. And I don't exactly intend to make it too easy for him on the trail back to Fort Smith." Bass Reeves winked at Larry Durham. "I ain't all that forgivin'."

THE END

Behind THE BIXBEE BREAKOUT

So how'd you like it? Pretty exciting stuff, right? At least I hope it was as exciting for you reading it as it was for me writing it. And now we get to the part where I tell you what I think is the boring stuff: what was my inspiration for writing the story, the research I did...blah blah blah yadda yadda yadda. Still, I understand there are those of you who enjoy all that so let's get right into it.

The Bass Reeves story I wrote for the previous volume was one I derived a great deal of satisfaction from as it was the first "straight" western I'd ever written. Oh, I've written four of five weird westerns and while they were a whole lot of fun to write it was always in the back of my mind that I couldn't really say I'd written a western until I wrote one that didn't have the crutch of fantasy elements to fall back on to keep the story moving. So I wrote "A Town Called Affliction" and it was pretty well received, I thought. But the real test is to pull off the same trick a second time. Which is why I wanted to write another Bass Reeves story. This one a little more action oriented than the first one.

I was inspired by two of my favorite westerns; "El Dorado" and "Rio Bravo" which are pretty much the same movie, separated by seven or eight years. In both of them, John Wayne, assisted by a motley crew including drunken lawmen (Dean Martin in "Rio Bravo", Robert Mitchum in "El Dorado"), cantankerous old coots and cocky young gunslingers attempts to hold onto a prisoner while his prisoner's gang attempts to break him out. If you've never seen either one, get yourself Blu-Rays of both and make it a double feature.

The concept is a fun one and appealed to me and it's one that has influenced a whole lot of stories, novels and movies. John Carpenter cites "El Dorado" as one of the major influences on his "Assault On Precinct 13"

178

and there's strong evidence that "Attack The Block" and "The Nest" were also influenced by those two westerns. So when it came time for me to write another Bass Reeves story, one that had more action to it (and going on the concept that great artists steal) I said why not? and crafted a story whereas Bass and Co. have to hold onto a prisoner against superior odds, assisted by a motley crew.

Will I be writing another Bass Reeves story? I hope to be able to. As the life and legend of Bass Reeves has become more popular in recent years and more people have discovered exactly how extraordinary a character he truly is, the opportunities for crafting more stories about him have grown. So you guys keep on readin' 'em and I (along with many other talented writers) will keep writin' em.

DERRICK FERGUSON is from Brooklyn, New York where he's lived most of his life. Married for 25 years to the wonderful Patricia Cabbagestalk-Ferguson who lets him get away with far more than is good for him. His interests include old radio shows, classic pulps from the 30's/40's, comic books, fan fiction, Star Trek, pop culture, science fiction, animation, television and movies...oh yeah...*movies.* He currently the co-host of the podcast ***BETTER IN THE DARK*** http://betterinthedark. podomatic.com where his partner Thomas Deja and he rant and rave about movies on a bi-weekly basis.

His primary love is reading and writing. He has written four books to date: ***Dillon And The Voice of Odin,*** his love letter to classic pulp action/ adventure with a modern flavor. ***Derrick Ferguson's Movie Review Notebook*** and its sequel ***The Return of Derrick Ferguson's Movie Review Notebook. Diamondback Vol I: It Seemed Like A Good Idea At The Time***, a spaghetti western disguised as a modern day gangster/crime thriller. For information on how to purchase them, please visit the Pulpwork Press website:

http://www.freewebs.com/pulpworkpress/

Anything else you'd like to know about me, check out my Live Journal: http://dferguson.livejournal.com/

What's Come Before:

BASS REEVES
FRONTIER MARSHAL

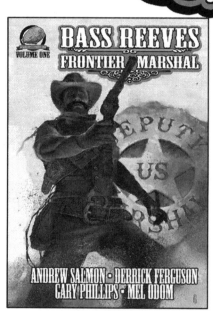

BASS REEVES
FRONTIER MARSHAL

VOLUME ONE

ANDREW SALMON · DERRICK FERGUSON
GARY PHILLIPS · MEL ODOM

FROM AIRSHIP 27

A WESTERN LEGEND COMES TO LIFE
FEATURING RIP-ROARING, WILD-WEST STORIES BY:
GARY PHILLIPS, MEL ODOM,
ANDREW SALMON
& DERRICK FERGUSON

PULP FICTION FOR A NEW GENERATION!
FOR AVAILABILITY: AIRSHIP27HANGAR.COM

AN AIRSHIP 27 PRODUCTION

Made in the USA
Columbia, SC
25 July 2017